M000014926

Girl Sailing Aboard the Western Star

RA ANDERSON

Girl Sailing Aboard the Western Star

Copyright © 2019 by RA Anderson, My Favorite Books Publishing Company, LLC.

All characters and events in this book, other than those clearly in the public domain, are fictitious and any resemblance to real persons, living or dead, is purely coincidental.

All rights reserved. No part of this publication may be reproduced, distributed, or transmitted in any form or by any means, including photocopying, recording, or other electronic or mechanical methods, without the prior written permission of the publisher, except in the case of brief quotations embodied in critical reviews and certain other noncommercial uses permitted by copyright law.

https://ra-anderson.com/
myfavoritebookspublishingco@gmail.com

My Favorite Books Publishing Company, LLC.
Kingston, Georgia USA

Ordering Information:

Quantity sales. Special discounts are available on quantity purchases by corporations, associations, and others. Orders by U.S. trade bookstores and wholesalers. For details, contact the publisher at the address above.

Editing by The Pro Book Editor
Interior and Cover Design by IAPS.rocks
Sketches by Hannah Jones

ISBN: 978-1-950590-03-2

  1. Main category—YOUNG ADULT FICTION/Coming of Age
  2. Other category—YOUNG ADULT FICTION/Epistolary (Letters & Diaries)
First Edition

To Mom and Dad,
and a thank you to Darryl for not tossing me overboard!

PREFACE

Hello, I am Annie! This is my journal, and my stories are real! The original handwritten journal has been lost, misplaced, or thrown away. However, before it vanished, I had typed most of it into a Word document because the ink and pencil were fading and I wanted to keep the memories someplace safe. The places we traveled and all of the events are true; however, several entries were half-written. I can only assume I had headed out on another adventure or was hiding the journal from my brother, but I tried to fill in the gaps with what I do remember.

In this sailing journal, I, as a young girl, compare the Pacific Ocean to the Atlantic, plus describe how I coped with missing my animals and our California ranch. This journal reminded me of all the land adventures I had while living in California and all of our adventures on the Pacific and Atlantic oceans. While I was reliving my adventures as I typed them out, I decided to share them all with you.

This was a trip of a lifetime, experiences no one can experience again, unless someone sets sail using only "old school" navigational tools and equipment from the late '70s. We had cassette players—no cell phones, computers, satellite, not even a television. It was a different time, but it made me the person I am today, filled with appreciation even for the small stuff in life and full of curiosity for life and adventures. It made me aware of the importance of our environment. It's the only world we have—there are no do-overs. My only regret today is that I wish there had been sunscreen, because unfortunately, I have battled skin cancer for the past ten years. But thankfully, they keep finding it early and cutting the darn cancer growths out.

This was our adventure told through my twelve- and thirteen-year-old eyes.

Come sail away with us aboard the *Western Star*.

⟩⟩⟩ KEEP OUT! PRIVATE! ⟨⟨⟨

No one is allowed to read this! I will never let
it fall into the hands of anyone besides myself,
especially not my brother DJ, who seeks me out
just so he can torture me.

This journal is for my eyes only!

If you are reading this now, you must
immediately

PUT IT DOWN...NOW!

and never pick it up

again

or you WILL suffer

serious consequences.

Oh, you will suffer!!!
Especially you, DJ!

CHAPTER 1

LEAVING IT ALL BEHIND

IT WAS NORMAL FOR DAD to fly across the country for a week or two on business trips to antique shows and auctions, so when he was gone in May of 1979, DJ and I didn't think anything of it. In retrospect, we should have asked why he was going on a business trip when he had sold his antique store. But it was May, and we were busy! DJ was finishing up his sophomore year of high school, surfing, skateboarding, and training for his motorcycle races. I was totally excited about sixth grade summer camp and then heading to Crabtree Farms in Kentucky for the horse show season, where I showed horses all summer. So, when Dad came home and slapped some pictures down on the kitchen table before dinner, DJ and I glanced at them and wondered why we needed a larger sailboat. Our sailboat, the *Sharon Ann*, was perfect for our weekend sailing trips to Catalina and holidays down to Cabo San Lucas.

And then the news shook us like an unexpected 8.0 California earthquake.

"DJ, Annie, come into the kitchen, I have something to tell you both. In August, we are all moving onto this fifty-three-foot sailboat and sailing down to the Caribbean," Dad announced while pointing at the sailboat's picture sitting on the table.

Whatcha talkin' 'bout, Willis? I thought as DJ and I sat in silence. *He didn't even ask us!*

Trying to smile, Mom softly added, "Annie, the animals will be shipped to our new farm in Kentucky and everything else will be sold. We will buy new furniture and things when we get there."

I wanted to ask where we would go to school, but Mom answered before anything came out of my mouth.

"We have hired a tutor for both of you. DJ and Annie, you both will be doing next year's schoolwork on the boat while we travel to The Bahama Islands, the Caribbean, and the Virgin Islands," Mom said matter-of-factly.

DJ got up from the table and stomped to his room, slamming his door hard enough to shake the entire house. Upset by DJ's ruckus, my cat, HoneyBear, jumped from my lap, and Stella and Jamie, Mom's dogs, trotted over to her. I sat there feeling sick and then tried to leave the table, but Dad ordered me to sit. As he walked out the kitchen door, I figured he was going to speak with DJ.

I looked across the table at Mom, feeling more uncomfortable than I had ever felt in my life. I had the urge to run, but couldn't. I finally felt able to speak, so I asked where all of our animals were going to be—the horses, ponies, dogs, cats, rabbits, guinea pigs, sheep, goats, and HoneyBear? I wanted to know!

"Annie, most of the horses and ponies will be shipped as soon as we sell this place or when we get to Kentucky. The dogs, my cat, and HoneyBear will be sent with the horses. Everything else will be sold or given away. Oh, and one of HoneyBear's kittens can come on the boat with us, and you get to pick which one," Mom said, looking down at her hands.

Leaving HoneyBear but taking her kitten is supposed

to cheer me up or make me feel better, but it doesn't! I haven't cried so many tears...well, since Grandma Ruth died. I feel so weak and so tired, so powerless and alone, at the thought of all my best furry friends in the world soon vanishing from my life.

Everything was being taken from me. My home, California, my best friends, my pets. I don't know who to talk to nor what to say, but I know I don't want to leave. This was forever, and I would never see...I think I am going to hurl.

I have a lump in my throat, and my eyes are filled with tears every time I think of my near future.

I guess all I can do is write in my new journal while getting through each day as if on autopilot.

AUGUST 9, 1979

Dear Journal,

I am too old for a diary. I am twelve-and-a-half years old. However, with all the crazy stuff going on in my life, I feel I have to jot it all down, or it may explode inside me. I need a friend to talk to. To tell—things. Dude, I have no one to share with...or at least I won't have anyone in a matter of days.

AUGUST 15, 1979

Dear Journal,

Why does every day feel like the last?

AUGUST 18, 1979

Dear Journal,

After my ride on Dolly, I hugged her neck and cried. She nudged me and wiped my tears with her muzzle. I took a deep breath in to remember her smell, and hugged her shoulder to remember the feeling. I hope she remembers me!

AUGUST 20, 1979

Dear Journal,

My world feels upside down, but maybe this happens to all twelve-year-old kids. Maybe it was the shock of my mother's near-death experience or Dad selling his antique business and needing something new in his life. What did DJ and I do for this to happen to us, or an even better question: How can we change our parents' minds?

The problem: We can't!

AUGUST 23, 1979

Dear Journal,

Goodbyes are hard. No, they are impossible and horrible!

AUGUST 24, 1979

Dear Journal,

Our bags are packed, and boxes are lined up around my room. Some are labeled Annie/KY and some are not. These are the boxes that are not making the journey across the country. It's just stuff, but it's the farm animals that I wonder about. Who will make the trip, who will be heading off to new homes? I can't even imagine my life without them all. Mom says most of mine will be shipped. Most? Who?

AUGUST 25, 1979

Dear Journal,

Move postponed! Because of a hurricane forming in the Caribbean. Mom is frantically calling the airlines and getting our flight rebooked to Florida. It's been a crazy day because we were due to leave in the morning and now we can't.

A few more days to ride and a few more days to sleep in my own bed with HoneyBear—this was truly a prayer answered.

SEPTEMBER 11, 1979

Dear Journal,

Do I write Dear Journal every time I start writing or just start writing a new section or paragraph? Or should I say Diary? At first, this sounded like a kid thing, but sailors keep diaries as their logbooks, with personal notes and thoughts. I guess with DJ being so snoopy, I will call it a journal but write it like sailors do in their logbooks, with a date and time for each new entry.

SEPTEMBER 12, 1979
WESTERN AIRLINES FLIGHT FROM SAN DIEGO TO MIAMI

I turned my face toward the window of the airplane, trying to hide the tears streaming uncontrollably down my cheeks. My journal is the only thing I have left. That sounds weird, but being ripped away from everything normal is weird!

Mom and DJ are getting settled in for our long flight to Miami. It's more like Mom is fidgeting, and DJ is kicking his bag under the seat in front of him. I rested my forehead against the small, oblong-shaped window until the vibration started and jet exhaust filled the cabin as we began to make our way from the gate to the runway. I don't know if I am nauseous from the smell of the exhaust or the fact that we are leaving <u>everything</u> behind. This is GETTING REAL.

The engines are growing louder, and the plane is vibrating my seat, the tray tables, and the storage bins above. The plane is bouncing me around, which just reminds me of an excited racehorse about to jump out of the starting gate at the Del Mar racetrack. I wonder if I will ever see another race at that track.

The plane is facing down the runway, so I think we are ready for takeoff. Then the G-force causes my whole body to sink into the back of my seat, vibrating and shaking. The challenge is in keeping my head from flopping back against the seat so I can write, so I'm going to look out the little window until this part is over.

7:00 A.M.

As our plane gained altitude, we turned, and we are now heading east. I looked out the window toward the north. My eyes followed Interstate 5 north in search of our ranch that's located just south of Rancho Santa Fe and west of Del Mar. The land below us was a blank slate, a mass of empty land, with no buildings, but I can see the miles of lima bean fields stretching from the hills to the new golf course to the road near the Del Mar racetrack. I saw the edge of La Jolla, from the buildings to the rolling hills. Cool, I located my first grade school, La Jolla Country Day. The only thing I saw after that was Black Mountain, which was off in the distance. Fading away—faster and faster the higher we climb. I tried not to blink. All I wanted to do was memorize the coastline, the mountains, all of it! I don't know when or if I will ever come, or go, back home. I feel numb. My eyes are burning, and I can't see what I am writing…I'll be back.

While the plane took off, I stared out the window and said my last goodbyes to San Diego and all the wonderful things I am leaving behind. Goodbye to our seventy-five-acre horse ranch. Goodbye to Vicky, my Shetland pony. Goodbye, HoneyBear, my calico cat. Goodbye, Amie and Laurie, my best friends.

My eyes still sting, even when I blink. I am really on a plane…I was hoping this was a bad dream!

I still don't understand why we couldn't bring HoneyBear along. Dad took HoneyBear's kitten, which we'd named BabyBear, with him when he left for Miami a couple months ago. Why couldn't he have taken HoneyBear, or both? HoneyBear has been with me since I was seven. Five whole years she has cuddled up to me in my bed and followed me around the house! No one will be there to pet her head and scratch her chin the way she likes me to. She will be all alone in the empty house and sure to think we died or she was abandoned with a caretaker to come feed her once or maybe twice a day. She's the best cat. When I was young, she let me dress her up with doll clothes—I only did that when I was young. One day when Mom and Dad were out, I wanted my two best pet friends to meet.

My room was on the second floor, so I walked Vicky up a flight of steps, down the hall, and into my room so they could meet. It was a success, but getting her to walk down the steps had been a challenge! Another time, HoneyBear woke me up early in the morning by biting my nose. I ran crying to Mom, so upset and needing her to explain to me why HoneyBear didn't like me anymore. Mom took me back to my room where HoneyBear was lying with several newborn kittens. It was amazing, and I was more than thrilled she still liked me. I was totally convinced Mom could fix anything! So, why wasn't she going to fix this and not make me go?

8:04 A.M.

I guess I needed a good cry and to watch out the window for a little while. I think I should write this down so that I will never forget. So here I am…

9:06 A.M.
FLYING OVER NEW MEXICO

Breakfast was served by the stewardess. We had eggs, bacon, and a soggy muffin. All the stewardesses are tall, very pretty, and look like they could all be in movies. I am wearing my nicest dress, the one I wore to the school dance, along with the white dress shoes, but leaving the stockings off might have been the wrong thing to do, as it's cold and sitting with my legs underneath me has cut off the circulation to my legs. I must go for a little walk to the lavatory to wake them up.

10:11 A.M.
SOMEWHERE OVER THE GULF OF MEXICO PASSING TEXAS

Vicky is a sorrel Shetland pony with a flaxen mane and tail. She and I met on my fourth birthday—what a gift! She and I have been cruising around as best friends ever since. I rode her for months in our riding arena before Mom let me ride off the ranch. Vicky and I played horse show as I shadowed Mom practicing on her show horses in the arena. The day finally came when Mom spoke down to me from up on her horse Fame and asked if I wanted to follow her out on a trail ride. Pure excitement ran straight through me like a lightning bolt. Mom led the way, and I followed on my sturdy steed, Vicky. We followed unnamed dirt roads for hours and hours, exploring the hills near our ranch. After several months of following Mom on these trail rides, she said she trusted Vicky and me to adventure off on our own. Since that day, we've enjoyed countless trail rides, making memories that I'll never forget.

But now that we've left the ranch…forever…

Who will give Vicky her favorite candy? Why she likes those hard, rainbow-colored, not-so-chewy Jujubes candies is beyond me. Maybe it's because they stick to her teeth and she can taste them for hours. Who will ride her out to Black Mountain or through the miles and miles of lima bean fields? I will miss riding through the half mile or so of strawberry fields, because not only did they smell heavenly, but when I wanted a snack, I could just slide off and pick a few. I wonder if anyone will ride her to the Del Mar's mudflats, just past the lima bean fields, headed toward the beach, or was our last trip OUR LAST TRIP for both of us? Sometimes the mudflats stunk of kelp drying up and dying on the beach—I might not miss that! The mudflats are fun to ride through because it's hard sand and, when cantering through them, trapped water from the ocean splashes up and cools us, which is so rad. Who will brush her and talk to her? Who will take her exploring in the eucalyptus groves and do the "Hi-yo, Silver, away!" move from the Lone Ranger, with Vicky taking off in a blazing gallop to the unknown? Who? And it shouldn't be anyone but me! As my pets see it, I probably simply bugged out, dropped off the planet…if they only knew. That is exactly how I feel—dropped off the planet.

There is one glimmer of light, though. Next summer, I will see them again. They will be moving to our new farm in Kentucky, traveling across the country. Mom assures me they will not be alone. I might not be there to greet them, but I will see them in another nine months or so. Not riding for that long is going to be torture. This trip, this move, gives a whole new meaning to heading into uncharted waters!

Thinking about them, writing about them, only makes my eyes sting again. I wonder what Vicky is doing now.

11:12 A.M.

FLYING OVER THE GULF OF MEXICO

DJ has fallen asleep next to me in the middle seat, but he could be faking it. If we were at home, he would be hiding in his room. He stays in his room for hours listening to his records. I know this because he plays them loud enough for all of us to hear all the way out at the barn, which is about 150 yards down the hill. It's either loud rock music, or he jumps on his motocross bike and races off where no one can find him. I've followed him toward

Black Mountain, him on his motorcycle and me on Vicky. It's not a race, but he loves to think so. It must be a sight: Vicky and I galloping as fast as we can, my thighs pressing into my little saddle pad as I keep balance and fight gravity pulling me backward. We race onward as if she and I could win this one. DJ only shifts into second gear and flies past Vicky and me, leaving us in a cloud of dust, yelling, "Eat my dust!" Fitting, isn't it?

Showing feelings or emotions isn't something DJ does. Maybe it's a guy thing, or maybe that's how all sixteen-year-old boys act. Well, he will be sixteen in two weeks. If he catches me crying, he pulls back and releases one of his famous Charlie-horse punches to my upper arm. Dag, those hurt. I truly believe my arms are damaged for life because of him. Lucky for both of us, his new handheld tape player came out about a month ago. It's called a Sony Walkman, and it plays cassette tapes. It doesn't have to be plugged into the wall because it uses batteries. Lucky for me, DJ's batteries are brand new, and the songs from his AC/DC tape will help him chill out for a while. I can hear "TNT" blaring from his headphones.

11:21 A.M.

SOMEWHERE OVER THE GULF OF MEXICO CLOSING IN ON FLORIDA

Mom and DJ swapped seats sometime; I guess I did fall asleep. I'm going to ask Mom to see the pictures of the new boat, our new home. Goodbye, *Sharon Ann*. Hello, *Western Star*.

12:03 P.M.
FLYING OVER TAMPA BAY BEACHES IN FLORIDA

Well, Mom seemed pleased. Smiling ear to ear, she started telling me all about the plans Dad has in store for us. She sounded super excited as she went on and on, but I didn't really want to hear any plans. I just wanted to cry. The pictures of the *Western Star* are beautiful. As I stare at them, I can't tell if I am more excited or nervous. The 53-foot Gulfstar Ketch is a cruiser-sailboat, much wider than the *Sharon Ann*. It seems to shine in the photograph, sailing through the really cool-looking turquoise-colored water of the Atlantic Ocean. The bright tricolored spinnaker sail seems to be pulling the boat effortlessly through the water, downwind, because that's when a spinnaker sail is used. I don't want to admit this, but it might be one of the prettiest sailboat pictures I have ever seen. The people in this picture look so tiny on the *Western Star's* deck. I wonder how they took these pictures from an airplane. I can't help but wonder what it will be like.

Does it matter? It will be awful without my friends. I can't help thinking about all of my furry friends, and another feeling of sharp pain hits my heart as my eyes sting again. I hope I don't smudge this paper. I've got to stop crying! I thought I would have run out of tears by now, but apparently not.

Mom is trying to tell me all kinds of stuff right now, but I don't want to hear any of it. I am figuring out that when I write, it's the only way to stop her from talking...I might have to pretend to write so I don't have to listen.

This stinks! My head is filled with what we have just left behind back west, now across the United States. In

California! The plane is descending—I guess this is it. A new life is waiting for us. Journal, I'll be back soon because I don't have anyone else to talk with and have run out of things to write to Laurie and Amie. Plus, after this brief stop in Miami, I am not sure if I can mail any letters. If only I could train a carrier pigeon to fly a note from our new boat in The Bahamas and the US Virgin Islands to southern California. We didn't leave an address for them to write me because the *Western Star* doesn't have an address! A carrier pigeon would be the only way to find us! Why do I feel like I am in a never-ending, very bad dream?

4:39 P.M. (TIME CHANGE!)
CAB RIDE TO CATCH FLIGHT TO BIMINI, THE BAHAMAS

This day will not end! A painfully boring flight, but at least Western Airlines has direct flights to Miami from San Diego. Then we had to hurry to catch our next flight at a different airport! We had to rush to pick up our bags and dash to catch a cab, and if only we were allowed to wear shorts and tennis shoes on airplanes, we could have sprinted faster. Dock shoes, tennis shoes, and flip-flops are all we wear, but I had to wear this stupid dress with dress shoes that I will never wear again. Thank goodness Mom didn't make me wear stockings. Who was the dude who made a dress code for flying?

Boots! I even miss my boots! I had to leave my boots at home. I am assuming they will be given away since they won't fit by the time I get to Kentucky. If I am not at the beach, I live in my boots. Once I was walking down the hill to the barn and went over what I thought was a stick, and luckily, I had my boots on, because it was a rattlesnake! True story! I thought of something that I will not miss—the snakes!

My writing is a mess because the cabbie is driving like a madman. Mom seems to be feeling better, but the rush at the Miami airport was probably not good for her. She looks white—whiter than normal. After her surgery a few months ago…it's been a slow recovery. Leaving California was doctor's orders. Mom and Dad didn't tell us that, but I overheard her say it to someone at a horse show. How could DJ and I fight that? She was always sick in California.

DJ and I were only allowed to bring a medium-sized duffle bag each because there would be no extra room on the boat. We really didn't need much—swimsuits, shorts, underwear, a couple pullovers, T-shirts, PJs, one light jacket, flip-flops, and deck shoes. Our schoolbooks were sent ahead with Dad, and anything else needed was purchased in Miami before he sailed to Bimini. I am not sure why he didn't wait for us in Miami, but I overheard him say something about making sure the boat was ready for us.

Mom thinks we might miss our flight. Later!

5:40 P.M.

ONWARD TO BIMINI, THE BAHAMAS

You won't believe what we are flying on to get to Bimini—a seaplane! It is scary, exciting, awesome, terrifying, and so totally cool! At the Miami Seaplane Base after we checked in, we were rushed to the dock, and I was practically tossed onto the floating plane. The seas were getting rough, and the chances of our being able to take off were getting slimmer by the minute. After everyone boarded, we instantly got bumped around by the waves. I'm not sure when I stopped breathing, but I think I held my breath until we were safely in the air. On takeoff, water was splashing the windshield. I shut my eyes and thought, *this may be the end.* It felt like the plane couldn't lift off, like the water was hanging onto us. Like a bird that had caught too big of a fish and couldn't take off. Louder and louder the engines roared, and the plane began to jolt and bounce. We bounced up and down and then a little left to right. For a moment, I thought we were going down instead of up. I felt my stomach reach my chest. The engine grew louder, the plane lunged harder; there was one more hard bump, and we flew right out of the waves, finally becoming airborne.

When I was able to open my eyes after the takeoff, I noticed DJ and Mom holding the sides of their seats, so I wasn't the only one scared. As the plane lifted and my heart was in my stomach—well, now that I think about it, my stomach was left in Miami on the dock—the rush was totally awesome. Or, as DJ put it, "It was rad."

Did I say terrifying?! The seaplane was flown by this dude who looked no more like a pilot than I do—okay, maybe no more than DJ. The engines were so loud that my head ached with pain and my ears were ringing. My eyes hurt and stung too. I could feel my heart thumping and racing. I will never forget that plane ride.

All seemed calm, so I turned and peeked out the window. Though still feeling incredibly sad about leaving California, I found myself stunned by the beauty below us. The water was turning colors from one depth to the next, the farther we flew away from shore. Starting at the white beach as clear blue, it turned a brilliant aquamarine and then changed colors again to a deep royal blue. The Pacific Ocean was more of a navy blue, in which whales could disguise themselves and a line of kelp floated off the shoreline just past the waves, but that was our past. I am now looking down at our future. I watched the shoreline for as long as I could from this small window, as the people disappeared, then the palm trees, then the buildings, and finally the shoreline and the beaches were gone too. I saw nothing but blue! There was nothing to see except blue water and blue sky with small cumulus clouds spread out as far as my eyes could see.

DJ has his headphones on, and occasionally I hear tunes spilling from them over the howling sounds of the engine. He is so angry and mean—I can totally relate. We both are leaving behind friends. I am sure he will miss his motorcycles that he spent hours riding across the hills behind our house, and the skateboarding park and all those friends, but probably not the broken arms he's gotten skateboarding. Oh, and he plays racquetball! He was second in the state—the whole state of California—and this was only a few months ago. That has to bite.

Here I sit, writing...my friends. Saying goodbye to my house, my stuff, my things, my animals, and now, goodbye to the United States. I even miss school right now. I can't hold back the dumb tears I am trying to hide from Mom and DJ. I need to face the window because the floodgates have opened once again. I'm surprised I have water left to cry.

6:10 P.M.

FLYING OVER THE ATLANTIC OCEAN BETWEEN USA AND THE BAHAMAS

Staring out the window again, I see the tiny little speck of an island growing larger as the plane makes a slight turn. The shapes of palm trees, beaches, and a few small houses are forming. We start descending upon one of the Bimini

Islands in The Bahamas, and it starts taking shape the way you would picture a tropical island.

We are here.

6:30 P.M.
SEAPLANE DOCK, BIMINI, THE BAHAMAS

Unlike a regular airplane, on which the moment the wheels are on the runway, the engines seem to reverse and the brakes are applied, in the seaplane, the floats touched the water and suddenly it felt more like landing in a big, sticky mud puddle. The water rushed over the back windows of the plane and sprayed out from the floats like a fire hose, cushioning us to a slow glide but more like a slowly sinking downward feel than the usual landing of a regular plane. The engines sounded almost relieved as they slowed to a putter, and then we made a sharp turn toward the dock and glided in.

So far this trip has had at least one perk—we flew on a seaplane! It was way cool and at the same time beyond words. I can only describe it as if we had entered a movie scene. It was so surreal, like we were famous actors flying away, off into the golden sky. It was totally wicked flying in a seaplane, but I am so glad the flight is over. And it didn't change the fact that I don't like leaving California, our house, our animals, Vicky, HoneyBear, and my friends.

6:57 P.M.
THE WESTERN STAR COCKPIT, BIMINI, THE BAHAMAS

As I was getting off that little floating airplane, my dress was stuck to me! The material was pressed against my skin, soaking wet from the heat. Heat, almost steam like, no—it was steam! This climate has a thick, humid wet air that's kind of like breathing water. The heat seemed to melt my whole body like butter—nope, not butter… nasty, sweat dripping off me as if I had just stepped out of a shower. I was sweating so much it was totally gross.

My dad was standing next to Mom by the time I got off the plane. His smile reminded me of a little kid waiting to open a Christmas gift. His dark brown hair now has extra highlights, and he is so very tan. Darker than I have ever seen him in my whole life. He smiled ear to ear, lighting up the whole dock, he looked so happy. Right then was when I realized how happy this move made him. But no matter how happy he looked standing there—I still want to go home. I still want to wake up from this horrible dream and be back in California. And then his first words to me made me want to hurl and cry.

"Hey, Sunshine." Dad reached for me, and we hugged a sticky, hot hug.

It's so hot—I don't want anything touching me!

Dad seemed so excited to see us as he rambled on about the boat and his journey to Bimini from Miami. We piled our things into the dinghy he had tied up to the dock and then made our way skimming across the water, the muggy hot air blowing through my long hair and whipping it across my face as I eagerly looked at all the anchored boats. I was tired, and I guess this made me feel willing to see my new home—sort of. The first thing I wanted to do was see BabyBear. It had only been twelve hours since I'd said goodbye to HoneyBear, but a hug from her daughter would help me feel closer to her.

The *Western Star* became REAL as we pulled up beside her huge hull! I didn't want to go aboard. I didn't want to see my room. Oh, wait, my brother's room…our room…our cabin. I had pictured it in my mind, and it was dreadful. The cabin would be a small, windowless, dark cubby-sized room with slivers for beds. I was sure it was going to be like a small compartment or stall. No! Our stalls are 14x14, and I would have to say our whole boat isn't that big, so I was sure our cabin would be like a locker at school. These thoughts of our cabin were the only things I could picture along with the fact that I would have to hear DJ snore and smell his nasty boy smells and farts—*farts!* I'd be suffering for nine months or more. Gag me with a spoon!

I felt sick to my stomach and wished to be back home. When Dad repeated my name, I realized it was time—I had to climb aboard. Good thing, too, because my imagination was taking off to the great unknown.

My bottom lip quivered, and I had to hold back the tears and felt sick! But I held it in the best I could. When it was time to see how small our little cabin, our tiny space, really is—this space we will be sharing for…way too long—I thought, *One of us might have to go!* On the other hand, I needed to see what was in store for me, where I was going to spend the next nine months or so.

I was still planted on the edge of the dinghy and realized I was all alone. "All aboard!" my father called out again. My heart was in my throat, and my legs didn't want to work. At that moment, Dad offered his hand to me, and the only thing that motivated me to move was the thought of seeing BabyBear.

Dad lifted my 80 pounds up, and I grabbed the wire railing that ran the circumference of the *Western Star*. It was wobbly as I held it, but I made my way through the opening and onto the deck. I could feel my body shiver and shake, though I wasn't cold. My nerves had the best of me. The deck has a narrow walk along the wire railing wrapped all the way around the sailboat's deck. I hope it helps keep me from falling overboard when DJ tries to knock me off. I stepped into the cockpit and stood behind the captain's chair at the helm. I found my way to a bench seat on the far side, on the port side, and took in my new surroundings. Dad and DJ disappeared belowdecks with the last of our bags as I sat staring down at the galley, our kitchen. The hatch was like any you'd see on most other sailboats—it's our front door to the boat's living area. However, this hatch is larger than the one on the sailboat we just sold in San Diego. On the *Sharon Ann*, I remember hitting my head several times when walking up the ladder from below. Just thinking about it, I can feel the pain and bump now.

On a boat, left is not left and right is not right! When I was about five or six years old, I think, Mom taught me how to remember port is the left side and starboard is the right side. Port and left have four letters each, and the color associated with it is red—smaller than green, which is the color for starboard! Easy peasy. Sail folding, knot tying, and line rolling become daily chores, and so does cooking, cleaning, sanding the teak, and oiling the teak. Cleaning seems like it would be easy because of how small of a space it is, but it's not! Salt builds up on everything, and somehow dirt does too. Salt is horrible because it will rust or eat through everything, and because everything is basically wet all the time, there is mold everywhere if you don't wipe down and clean often. The wood that's not varnished has to be sanded down and new teak oil applied, and this is done more often than I would even think. So the chores are done by everyone, every day. Anchoring, handling sails, and navigation are everyday chores as well, but back on the *Sharon Ann*, I was too small to do the hard jobs. I could tighten a line with a winch and cleat it off, make sandwiches with Mom, secure below deck, and several other smaller jobs became my responsibility, but now, I would be helping with more. Even though it sounds like "work," I can't wait to help with the sailing part. It would bite if I had to sit around and do nothing and hear "you're too small" all the time.

COCKPIT, ONBOARD THE WESTERN STAR

As the sun disappears, it's hard to write, and my name being repeated several times from below brought me out of my thoughts; I decided to follow the voices. I turned to face the stairs and went below, as you say on a boat.

SEPTEMBER 12, 1979 – THE LONG TRAVEL DAY ABOARD THE WESTERN STAR

A familiar smell lingered…the smell of being below deck. It's not bad, but just like on the *Sharon Ann*, it's like no other smell I can compare it to. The scent of still-salty air is unmistakable. As I turned around from the ladder, I noticed how much bigger, wider, the *Western Star* is than our previous boat. We took the *Sharon Ann* on countless sailing trips down Baja California and to Catalina Island for weeks at a time, but we couldn't have lived on her for a year. Maybe we could have, but not very comfortably. Glancing around, I noticed several more differences right away.

Looking right to left, my eyes settled on the navigational station on the starboard side. Two small desks sat end-to-end along the wall, which was lined with navigational instruments. I had never seen some of the equipment before, but the sight of familiar nautical charts rolled up and stored above the desks, tucked away in a compartment, gave me some comfort. Nautical charts are a boat's most important tool. They show where a boat can go and what time to go with information about water depths, hazards, distances, and marker buoys. One day maybe Dad will teach me how to read them. To me they look like trying to read a foreign language for the first time. A new single side band and a VHF radio for talking to other boats or even ship-to-shore calls are mounted off to the side for easy access in case we have to use them for an SOS call. Hopefully we don't have to make an international Morse code distress signal any time while on the boat.

Across to the other side of her hull, on the port side, is the galley. It's much bigger than the *Sharon Ann's* galley, and it looks like I won't have to reach down into the deep icebox because we have a refrigerator and a freezer. Cool beans! It's much, much smaller than the refrigerator at home, but it's the biggest I've seen in a galley. Wait, I've never seen a refrigerator on a boat before. I opened the refrigerator to see what was inside and a sharp, "Keep the refrigerator door closed!" came as a bark from my dad. Then he came into the galley and pointed out that we have a freezer, a refrigerator, and another one, not as cold, for drinks. Three!

Since I was in the little hall between the engine room and the refrigerators, I wandered to the aft cabin to find BabyBear; the aft cabin is Mom and Dad's room. BabyBear remembered me and rubbed up against my hand faster than I could pet her. I picked her up and gave her a gentle hug, and she sniffed my face. I kissed her forehead like I used to kiss HoneyBear's. My heart felt like it was breaking all over again—this is HoneyBear's first night without me. As I loved on BabyBear, I glanced around the cabin. The aft cabin is totally awesome. It's the master room and takes up the whole stern area, the whole back end of the boat! Mom and Dad have their own head and a double bunk, a single bunk, and even a little sitting area. It was large for a cabin in a sailboat. They are using the extra bunk for storage. Bulk packages of toilet paper, paper towels, dried cereals, and tons of canned goods...all the extra supplies we need for our journey were lined across this bunk.

I put BabyBear down and walked back through the little hallway with the refrigerators I desperately wanted to open. No reason—just wanted to open them. I walked forward, toward the bow, or the front of the boat, for a better look at the living area, known as the saloon. There is a long couch on the starboard side and a dining table on the port side. Dad pointed out that the table folds down to a double bunk if needed, then he showed me the storage areas above the seats and grabbed a cushion from the couch, revealing larger storage compartments underneath the seats too.

As I explored the remainder of the boat alone, I noticed the wall near the table has a photo of the *Western Star* under sail. It's the same photograph Mom showed me on the airplane, but in a large frame bolted and secured to the wall. No fear of it falling off when the waves are high and the boat goes a-rocking!

As I took a few steps toward the bow, there's a very narrow and short hallway where four doors meet. The first door on the right is a folding door that hides a very small washing machine. All of the walls are teak wood, as is the dining table, and I am glad we won't have to sand and oil all of them because sheltered from the weather as they are, they should be good for a while—I hope. I noticed the table, like the *Sharon Ann's*, has little teak ridges called fiddles that are supposed to help stop things from sliding off when the boat rocks. Many plates of food were saved from falling on laps or onto the floor on the *Sharon Ann* during meals.

The other three doors are for the forward head, the V-berth, and the forecabin (forward cabin). This small little area makes a tight intersection. A no-passing-zone sign should be mounted on the wall!

The door on the starboard side is the door to the head, which is an extremely small bathroom, about the same size as the one on the *Sharon Ann*, maybe a little bigger. There's a tiny stand-up shower and a toilet alongside a sink. I could sit on the toilet, brush my teeth, and shower at the same time if I wanted. This is simply raunchy…a horrifying thought. I went inside and tried to hold my arms out straight but couldn't without touching the door or walls. There is a small porthole and a small vent—that's good because I am sharing it with three boys this time, including the first mate/tutor/cook. We were never on the *Sharon Ann* longer than two weeks, nor with this many people. As I approached the head, Dad entered and called for DJ. Then dad showed DJ and me how to use the electric flusher, and I figured at least if you hear the pump running, you will know to get out of the water!

The V-berth is a room in the very front of the boat is where captain John and first-mate/tutor/cook will be staying. I peeked inside and couldn't imagine both men staying in that small of a cabin. I guess it's just to sleep in. The beds meet together at the bow, making a V shape—thus its name.

Across the hall from the head, I inspected what was behind the third and last door. This door would be my room. WAIT—mine and DJ's room! DJ was already inside with the door locked. I wanted to find BabyBear again, wondering if she would sleep with me.

Finding her helped and didn't. I love having her here, but she makes me miss HoneyBear even more. Mom was going to bed, so she shooed me away, out of the aft cabin, and ordered me to go to bed. I scooped the kitten up from the extra bed in Mom and Dad's room, or cabin, kissed BabyBear goodnight, and scurried out of the aft cabin and made my way forward. Back at my cabin—*our* cabin—DJ wouldn't let me in. I knocked, grabbed the door lever, and shook at the door, trying to get inside. He was holding the door shut with his foot. After a minute, he opened the door just enough to punch my arm and then slammed the door shut. My arm was totally dead! The pain was horrible. I cried, and Mom yelled at me all the way from the aft cabin, this time ordering me to go to bed. This is was the first fight between DJ and me on the new boat, but it was more like a sucker punch, and then I was the one who got yelled at for fighting. I am sure this won't be the last fight aboard the *Western Star*. He is such a psycho!

9:00 P.M. EST
MY CABIN – OUR CABIN

It's not a bad dream, I am sitting awake on my bed; it only feels like a nightmare. DJ left, maybe he's on deck, but at least he's gone so I can get unpacked and go to bed.

My cabin's floor space is just large enough for the door to open in the tight standing area beside the bunks, with the bunks run in an L-shape, with two ends overlapping one another. The longer bunk, the bed DJ took, runs along the boat's hull, bow to stern. I was left with the shorter, higher bunk, the bunk that runs left to right, or port to starboard. I liked this bunk because when, or if, anyone opens the door, my bed was behind the door. I feel like I have a little more privacy than the other bunk. As far as it being the shorter bunk, I didn't mind that at all since I am almost five feet tall—when I tiptoe. I am able to see out of the little porthole from the top bunk too. It's not all that bad…no, it's horrible. It wouldn't be bad for a few days or even a couple of weeks, but it is really small…considering this will be a room that I have to share with my older brother for the next nine months or so. People say sailing can go from fun to frightening in less than a second. Well, sharing a cabin with DJ is terrifying from the very start.

It took me all of a minute to unpack my bag, and my belongings didn't even fill up my four drawers that are under my bed. It looks like my bed is on top of a dresser and is about the height of one too. I have to step on DJ's bunk to get onto my bed. Note to self: get on my bunk before DJ gets in bed or after he is asleep. There is a space alongside my bed where I just tucked my photographs, small knickknacks, and the notes I brought from Laurie and Amie. Hidden from sight but easy for me to get to while in bed.

Oh, I forgot to write about meeting Captain John and Bruce. Captain John seems quiet but was very nice. He has jet-black wavy hair and dark eyes and is dark-skinned, or very tan, possibly both. Bruce is the cook/tutor; he's a tall blond guy, a surfer-looking dude. Seems nice but didn't say much.

I am glad I can find places to write like up here in my bunk, at least until DJ comes in or maybe up on deck where I can see and hear someone approaching, but that will only work in the day.

Strange how cramped we are on the boat—yet I've never felt so alone.

Goodnight, John-Boy!

No answer…I am alone.

SEPTEMBER 13, 1979
BIMINI, THE BAHAMAS

So…yesterday was the longest day ever. I guess I'd thought this trip—this move—wasn't going to happen! Sharing a cabin with DJ is pure torture. He has already slammed the door into my back while I was unpacking and cut the cheese and ran out, holding the door shut to lock me inside with his stench. He's such a goon!

We have never liked having to share space. From the time I was really young, I can remember fighting him for space. Like the time we were in the back of our car traveling to Disneyland and Mom and Dad put a suitcase between us, hoping to keep us from fighting. DJ spent the whole time pushing the suitcase into me with his feet, making my space smaller and smaller and shoving me up against the car door. I cried and told Mom and Dad, and I was the one to get in trouble. We have such a love/hate, more hate than love, relationship. How will we survive this new life, in these tight quarters, for these nine long months? I can't find an alone place to even write. DJ has grabbed the journal and threatened to toss it overboard, but Mom saw and stopped him.

This trip must end!

CHAPTER 2

SETTLING IN

SEPTEMBER 16, 1979

ANCHORED NEAR THE MARINA, BIMINI, THE BAHAMAS

Getting settled in on the *Western Star* is the most anyone seems able to do today. The slow, constant rocking makes me fall asleep again and again, and I've been asleep most of the day. I hear Mom and Dad talking about heading to shore, to Bimini, for dinner.

Later!

7:45 P.M.

MY BUNK ON THE WESTERN STAR

We took the dinghy to shore and then walked on land for the first time since we arrived, September 12th. It was so strange! The ground felt as if it were moving, like I was still bobbing with the waves, because the perpetual movement of the *Western Star* was already embedded in my legs' muscle memory. My new sea legs needed a break—or I did. We walked up a slight hill on a bumpy sandy road for about thirty minutes, passing downed trees and debris left from the hurricane that had passed over The Bahamas a couple weeks ago. I remember hearing on the news that the storm had left many people homeless here and even in the US.

Luckily, Mother Nature had spared the local place Dad found. He thinks it is the coolest place ever and has eaten there almost every day. Something about a man named Ernest Hemingway hanging out here. I am not sure if that's a friend of Dad's or what, but maybe we will meet him. Dad doesn't meet a stranger, and I simply feel like hiding when new people are around. I don't know what other word to describe the way I feel when I meet someone new, but it's like totally painful.

We stopped in front of someone's house, and Dad walked up the steps and went right inside! I didn't realize it was a restaurant until the smell of sweet food came blowing out the front door. I hesitated before stepping inside, as I heard someone call Dad by name and then footsteps getting louder. As I entered, this Bahamian lady was hugging everyone, all eager and happy to meet us all. It's as if we were meeting family for the first time. We sat at a lone four-chaired table in the corner of the room.

Small unframed canvas paintings covered the walls. They were canvases splashed full of brilliant colors, each one showing island scenery, trees, beaches, the marketplace, dancing, and goombay drums and calypso bands. My favorite was of the lighthouse with the sun setting behind it. I also like the coconut tree that has rays of light coming out of each palm leaf. The people in the paintings always seem to be silhouettes alongside the brightest of colors, no matter what the scene. I wish we had paints on board. I could paint the sky and the sea. I could paint Vicky in her paddock, waiting for me to return, or HoneyBear hiding in my pile of stuffed animals on my bed. My grandmother Ruth bought me a paint set, but I am not an artist. I make stick men look bad. But it would have been fun to paint on deck.

I realized I had been looking at the art on the wall for a while and started looking around. The furniture was pieced together and painted brightly as well. When I was asked what I wanted to eat, I hadn't given the old piece of paper, the menu, a second glance. I couldn't decide what to eat and couldn't read the menu that fast. They have several things that I had never seen or heard of before. Living in California and traveling with my parents, I was familiar with tropical fruit and with all kinds of fish, but this place made me feel as if I had never been outside of my house, it was so different. The food sounds exotic. Even though The Bahamas are only about sixty miles off the coast of Florida, it's not Florida, and it definitely has its own vibe. Maybe it is like Florida, but really how different could California be than Florida? I also read who Ernest Hemingway is—or was. A picture of him hangs in a corner of the room, saying something like he spent time here while writing his books. Apparently, he was a famous author from the US. That's totally cool!

It was hard at first to understand what anyone was saying under the heavy accents. The natives are Bahamian and speak English, but they have a Creole—island—accent of some kind that is hard to understand. The owner asked if I wanted conch fritters, cracke' conch, or conch salad. I must have been staring at her for a minute with my mouth draped open by the time Dad chimed in. He explained that conch is the critter that lives in the huge conch shell, the shell you can put up to your ear and hear the ocean even years after it was taken from the ocean. I am super glad he didn't remind me that it's the slimy critter that appears to have one soft claw for pulling its body around the ocean floor, because I probably wouldn't have eaten anything, especially not a conch. But after all that, it wasn't the conch I was wanting to try. I actually had no idea what the nice woman said to me. I was warned the food is spicy hot, and I do like spicy hot Mexican food, so how different could this be? Dad ended up ordering for me, which made me crazy mad! I am not a kid! I can order for myself.

When dinner arrived, it too seemed bright in colors, especially yellow. I have to admit dinner was totally awesome! It was a different hot than any Mexican restaurant; it's hot like the food my grandmother from New Orleans made—it's creole hot! Dinner was awesome, but the best part was the pie Dad ordered after dinner. He didn't order a piece of pie. He ordered three whole pies to take back to the boat. One bite of the banana coconut pie and I wanted a whole pie for myself—totally a mouth full of wonderful!

My love for tropical fruits is probably from spending so much time on boats, or it could be from growing up in California. It's how we eat—fruit, nuts, vegetables, all of the time. At home, outside my bedroom window, there are rows of plum and apricot trees. When in season, I have to race the birds to these wonderful treats. Outside our front door was a huge kumquat tree. I love those sour little orange things. To me, they are better than any sour candy. My favorite is our pomegranate tree, down the hill toward our horse barns. I miss home! I even miss the time Vicky ran me into that branchy pomegranate tree, and I had a hundred scratches all over my body and branches stuck in my hair. Back to food—we eat the fruits and fish, or we don't eat at all. I heard that a thousand times from my mom. Tonight was no different. My parents wanted us to experience everything, and lucky for me, tonight included this pie. It's totally awesome! If Mom would let me, I would eat the whole pie by myself tonight.

Back at the boat, after dinner, I searched for BabyBear, curious if she's anything like HoneyBear. I really miss HoneyBear. Out of the seven kittens in the litter, BabyBear looks the most like HoneyBear. I hadn't seen or heard her since the first day on board, but I found her hiding behind the pillows on Mom and Dad's bunk. She looked comfortable taking her catnap. I didn't want to bother her, but I yearned to hold HoneyBear, and BabyBear was the next best thing. She seemed to remember me, but she was much more interested in her nap. I held her for a little while until Mom entered, then I put her down and decided to go to bed to write all of this down.

SEPTEMBER 18, 1979
BIMINI, THE BAHAMAS

The *Western Star* sounds like her belly is grumbling and her hull shakes when her diesel engine starts. The sound of heavy footsteps above me on deck startled me awake, and then the sounds of the steps got faster, almost as if someone was running up and down the deck. I can feel the engine was put in forward, and I can hear the anchor line being heaved-up up by the windless, which is the machine-driven winch. The anchor line is slapping against the inside of the hull in the anchor locker just in front of the V-berth. Now the chain is coming up, it's clanking in the anchor-locker, and we are on the move. Yep, the engine roared louder! I must get my swimsuit on and get up on deck! But first, a piece of pie for breakfast! Maybe?!?

9:00 A.M.

One pie is missing—and it wasn't me!

It's been hard to find a space where someone isn't being nosy. Plus, I tried to write but when Mom sees me with this notebook it reminds her of schoolwork, and I am then ordered to go start on my studies.

I had to start on something, so I chose to work on some math. That should be good for a while.

3:30 P.M.

SAILING FROM BIMINI TO NASSAU, THE BAHAMAS

I wondered up on deck and found a nice little spot on deck that I can lean back on the cabin and write finally, as no one is around. It's best to sit still and out of the way as the sails are hoisted and the boom is given some slack before the wind finds its mark and fills the mainsail. I feel a slight but noticeable heel as the *Western Star* leans slightly while the wind fills her sails and starts pushing us along. The engine cuts off, and the sounds of deckhands' footsteps settle as the jib is cleated and secured. The sounds of the sails being filled, much like a soft whip being popped, and the soft clinging of the wire stay hitting up against the mettle of the main mast, sounded somewhat like a sharp bell off in the distance.

I sit facing west as I watch the palm trees on Bimini sinking in our rear view as we follow the Providence Channel from Bimini to Nassau.

All the things I had overheard my parents talking

about while at home in California are starting to make sense to me now.

Dad left California about two months before us to prepare the boat. He hired Captain John and a first mate who could cook and tutor, Bruce. The four of us and two hired shipmates make the boat seem even smaller than the *Sharon Ann*. In Miami, Dad had to purchase supplies for the kitchen, food, bedding, towels, toiletries, and most importantly, the new navigational tools and equipment. He even attended classes and earned his captain's license so that he now is an official captain of our boat, but Captain John knows these waters and will be a "peace of mind" for our safety in these waters that we haven't traveled before. Dad must have been really busy those two months in Miami, Florida, and I'd thought he was on a vacation without us.

So, this is the *Western Star*. She's larger than the *Sharon Ann* by eight feet in length, but her girth—

Sorry, I slipped back to the words I use with my horses. Tack is the bridle and saddle and equipment used when riding or working with horses, and a girth strap is used to fasten a saddle around the midsection of a horse. I have no idea why I am describing this to my journal because no one will ever read this. I guess I am bored and rambling on, and I miss my horses! Anyway, I meant to say, beam.

The *Western Star's* width is her beam, and it's about ten feet wider than the *Sharon Ann's*, allowing a lot more room in the living quarters. Her large hull is white with blue trim that I didn't notice in the photograph, or I don't remember it. She has two masts, the main mast and the mizzen mast, unlike the *Sharon Ann's* single main mast. And there are bright blue custom canvas sail covers and matching storage container covers up on the raised deck area. The mainsail's canvas cover is being removed now as we motor away from Bimini. All of the teak is stained, all of the brass has been shined, and the chrome is glistening in the sun, actually blinding me when the sun hits it just right. I could tell Dad and the crew, Captain John and Bruce, had worked hard on the boat preparing it for our arrival and trip ahead. The truth is, I like having Captain John and Bruce on the boat; they keep DJ busy, and he hasn't wanted to show them that he's a pesty brother. I have to admit this—sitting here is kind of cool. The wind is warm, the colors from the ocean to the sky are vivid, and this boat sails nice. I guess the eight-foot difference and having a bigger beam makes the *Western Star* sail like a luxury cruiser. It's peaceful on deck, and it looks like everyone is finding their place.

5:00 P.M.

SAILING BETWEEN BIMINI AND NASSAU, THE BAHAMAS

I hadn't learned or even heard much about The Bahama Islands, or the Atlantic Ocean, or the Caribbean, or the Caribbean Islands…nor did I try to learn anything. I was sure this move wasn't going to really happen, so I didn't care. Denial, but here we are!

We spent so much time on the West Coast, traveling down Baja California on the *Sharon Ann*, I figured this wasn't going to be much different. As I look out past our sails, along the water…this is incredibly different. The Pacific Ocean is a deep dark blue, with lots of kelp floating off the shoreline that smelled bad depending on the time of year, and the water is always cold, sometimes ice cold. During our sailing trips down Baja California, we would see pods of orca whales. They would swim alongside our hull while we were under sail. Once there were so many that they scared Dad, and I had never seen him scared before—not like that day. Pods of porpoise would spend hours splashing and jumping in our bow's wake, and that was always fun to watch, especially from the bow of the boat, but I don't know if we will see any here. On the *Sharon Ann*, Dad would let me sit on the bow and watch the porpoises play as long as I stayed on top of the raised deck where he could see me. We used to follow the Baja shoreline for miles and miles where we would see tall cliffs and white beaches, and some beaches peeked out from behind the cliff's shadows. I loved the dark black cliff formations and the waves' white foam crashing against them. There the air was always cold, so wearing jackets and long-sleeved shirts was a must. The odor of the kelp was sometimes stinky, but at the same time it gave me the feeling of being on the boat, and being on the boat was when everyone was happiest together. The ocean was dark, mysterious, and cold, and the seas were rough with huge waves and swells. With every swell our little sailboat sailed through, the wind would carry cold ocean spray to our deck, salting us as if it were seasoning us for her next meal. Here, in the Atlantic Ocean, the water seems calmer, and the breeze is cooling us from the thick heat, but nothing but a swimsuit is needed. I would welcome a splash of cold right now. We are NOT in the Pacific Ocean anymore—this is totally different!

A sudden command was given for a tack, so everyone jumped to it and quickly accomplished the mission. About an hour later, another command was given, and we tacked again. When wind is coming from the direction that we would like to travel, it's called a headwind; basically, the wind direction is in our face. Instead of traveling in a straight line, we must zigzag back and forth, moving forward a little at a time. When we turn the boat back to the other direction, we tack. To tack, the boat is turned or pointed into the wind. This allows us to switch the sails to the other side. If the boom isn't switched slowly, it can really bang someone hard. This, and because so many people bang their heads on it while sitting in the cockpit, is why some people call the boom a boom-bang. The jib sail is a sail in front of the mast. There are two lines tied to the bottom back part of the sail, running to both sides of the boat. One is untied, and the line is loosened enough to allow the sail to be guided to the other side by tightening the other line attached to the opposite side. Then both lines are secured. If you tacked without doing this, the jib sail would could get stuck in the boat's rigging (all the lines and wires holding up the mast), and the jib wouldn't work. After the sail lines are secure the sailboat is slowly turned so sails can fill, and the lines are then tightened and adjusted so we can sail onward. It takes forever to get where we want to go in a headwind. Especially when you see land, because it doesn't feel like we are making any headway. Because we keep going left and right—back and forth. I was just thinking about only having one jib line—I could see DJ walking a line around the rigging wires with a line while the jib sail flapped in the wind, and he would have to run the line back to the other side, wrap the line around the winch, and winch it in. He would have some words—colorful words, I bet.

7:00 P.M.
DINNER AT SEA

Watching someone cook in the galley while under sail is entertaining, until they notice you and then you are to join in the fun. I helped Bruce cut the carrots up and diced an onion while sitting at the table. He did all the hard work, cooking with one hand holding on, and he managed to lean up against the counter and use both hands until he needed to move. We ate in shifts, leaving two on watch and the other four to eat first. So Mom, Dad, DJ, and I sat down and ate first, discussing how our first day at sea had gone and what time we should see land in the morning.

7:00 A.M.

SAILING AT SUNRISE

I sat on the raised cabin for a few minutes, then made my way closer to the bow and sat with my back up against the raised cabin—the place directly above the V-berth. I kept looking forward at the bowsprit and knew that was my destination. The bowsprit is about four feet long and maybe two feet wide and has a secured railing that wraps around the front and sides; this is what anchors the front of the wire railings that run on both sides and around the deck. It feels as if I am in a horse corral, fenced in on the boat. I crawled up to the bowsprit and still heard nothing coming from the cockpit. Slowly, I inched my way onto the bowsprit. I fit perfectly between the anchor cradle and the railing but in front of the anchor windlass. I sat holding on to the railing with my legs crossed underneath me until my legs fell asleep. When I had to move them, I dangled them down off the bowsprit and felt the spray of water on my legs and feet. DJ showed up, and I was assuming it was to tell me I had to move, but instead he plopped down on the other side of the bowsprit and copied me. It was a good feeling—I am not sure if it was because DJ and I were breaking a rule we didn't know existed or what, but it was super cool dangling our legs off the front of the boat.

In the bow's wake, a dolphin appeared and then two and then several. We were so close to them that when the bow dipped down into a wave's trough, pitching the boat's bow up and down, it almost felt as if we could touch a dolphin with our feet. We were playing in the new morning sun.

As the sun rises higher in the sky, the water's aquamarine color changes shades. The *Western Star*'s bow splashes through the swells, and as we travel into the deeper waters, a new color is shown. Off in the distance, the water is darker near the horizon, meeting up with the light blue sky. There's hardly a cloud in the sky today. This makes me wonder if it will be like this every day.

2:00 P.M.

SAILING

We had lunch, then DJ and I found our way back to the bowsprit. Looking down into the water, it is the best seat on the *Western Star*! DJ and I started noticing the bottom of the ocean seemed a bit close but figured it was because the water was so clear. We could see fish, several shapes and sizes of coral, lots and lots of sand, and seagrass beds…it was amazing, and a bit strange. It was more than strange, the fact DJ was sitting next to me and we were not fighting and he hasn't tried to push me off the boat yet.

DJ and I heard Dad's stories of ships sinking in The Bahamas because of the coral and sand reefs, and I don't want to be one of them. Coral is one of the sharpest living animals on Earth, who discrete—kind of like poop—limestone; this is what helps builds their massive reefs. While boogie boarding in Hawaii one vacation about a year ago, I sliced my left foot open on flattened-shaped coral that looked like rock, and with my right foot stepped on a sea urchin. That was a one-two punch that hurt like crazy, and I ended up in the hospital. That wasn't my favorite vacation! The hospital wasn't much help with the sea urchin, because if you try and pull a sea urchin needle out, they just break off and go deeper—in my case, that would have been into my feet and between my toes. As the nurses cleaned out the coral, they, being native to Hawaii, told me how corals are animals. Strange, I know! The nurses were nice, and they cleaned as much as they could and well, at least they made sure I wasn't going to die. My uncle carried me around the entire time we were in Hawaii. Needless to say, I respect coral now and couldn't thank my uncle enough for the piggyback rides. It baffles me that coral isn't a mineral or a plant. I have to keep reminding myself that it's a delicate animal. Delicate—tell that to my damaged feet! I could only imagine what it could do to the hull of a sailboat. Dad said there are several sunken ships in the area, including pirate ships too. I don't want one of the reefs to claim the *Western Star*.

A loud beeping sound from the cockpit made DJ and me both cover our ears, but we also wanted to know what it was. We both looked back at the cockpit and noticed Mom and Dad looking over the port side of the boat, so we decided to go see what in the world was going on.

Dad had purchased a new device called a sonar that was installed underneath the boat, somewhere on *her* keel, and it "sees" under the water for us. The sonar sends out pulses of sound waves, and the instruments record the time it takes for the sound waves to come back to the boat from whatever they encounter, like the sandy ocean floor, or coral, or a shipwreck. The sonar was making a smooth, continuous pinging sound. If the sound breaks, slow and steady, something is close but not too close. When the beeping sounds become louder and more repetitious, something is extremely close to our hull or keel. Again, that something could be sand, rock, coral, or a shipwreck. There is a reef here called the Devil's Backbone that claimed several pirate ships, and I am not sure how many ships it's claimed since those pirate days.

Besides the sonar, our backup, or safety depth readers, are the two depth finders. We had depth finders on board the *Sharon Ann* and we are used to reading them, but never were we in waters this shallow. The depth finders give us readings of the depth directly beneath our hull, or on the keel, in feet. I believe Dad set it to feet, not meters or fathoms, but haven't double- checked that yet. If it's not in feet, doing the math conversions will stink! It's one of those things you can't guess at—nor do you want to out here.

A flash of fear caught me off guard when I heard Captain John say, "Strike the sails and back the jib!" Snapping back to it, I quickly helped drop the sheets *(sail lines),* and Captain John heaved to (turned the boat into the wind). We immediately heard the diesel engine start and gurgle and then suddenly, she slammed into reverse. The engine shook the hull with force and jolted us all from where we sat or stood. I could hear something down belowdecks crash to the floor and hoped it wasn't Mom.

The coral DJ and I saw earlier was actually and totally too close. I was not sure what our draft was at the time, how low this boat sits in the water, but if coral hits our hull or keel, we are doomed like the pirate ships that sunk here in the 1700s and 1800s. We are in the Bermuda Triangle! We could sink and disappear without a trace.

DJ and I secured the sails by tying them down and wrapping lines. We could hear Mom shouting out numbers while the sonar spazzed out. The beeping was starting to drive me bananas. I had asked Dad what our draft was, and he said about 4.6 feet...so if the coral are above five feet, this could be a disaster!

I couldn't stop thinking, *Well, this was a fun short vacation. Now let's go home.*

And then, *We didn't sink! We're sailing*—again.

CHAPTER 3

AUTOPILOT

SEPTEMBER 19, 1979

SITTING ON DECK, ANCHORING OUT, NASSAU, THE BAHAMAS

Today we ended up sailing past and over several more sandbars, pure white sand under the lightest aquamarine shades of water. It was crazy that one minute we could be in twenty feet of water and then only have three feet under our keel faster than we could blink an eye. The sandbars are like beaches stretched out in the ocean, but without trees, houses, or even an island, for that matter.

As we sailed into Nassau, we passed a really cool lighthouse sitting on the end of the island to mark the low-lying key, or the shallow sandbar hidden from boats. This is one of the most dangerous reefs in The Bahamas, and every boat passes it coming into Nassau. We watched the reef carefully as we cruised into the canal. Palm trees near the edge of the island, coconut trees, and emerald-green thatch palms were all waving at us as if celebrating our arrival. What? I can pretend to be funny in my own journal! I have to go roll lines.

Later!

NASSAU, THE BAHAMAS

In my bunk getting away from everyone. Rolling lines and tethering sails isn't bad, but when you have more than three people telling you different ways to do something it gets more than annoying.

My door is shut, trying to shut out the men on the boat, but unfortunately, I can hear them, everyone, through the walls, through the deck, and outside the door. This cabin feels claustrophobic. I am not feeling like writing, or doing anything, for that matter.

SEPTEMBER 20, 1979
NASSAU, FUELING DOCK, THE BAHAMAS

We are motoring to the docks for some quick supplies and to top off our 400-gallon fuel and 400-gallon freshwater tanks before we head out. Mom and Dad probably are going to go find a cake and gifts for DJ as well. The *Western Star* holds 400 gallons each of fuel and water. It sounds like a lot of water, but actually, for five people, it's super easy to use up 100 gallons a day. Dad said a family of five at home would use over 400 gallons per day, without using a washing machine, a dishwasher, or filling a bathtub. Dad made sure DJ and I knew all of this information—his way of warning us not to overuse or waste water. I have no clue how other boats could last without a water maker, which Dad said turns saltwater into fresh water somehow, but if I ask him how it works, he will tell me in detail whether I want to hear it or not. So I am tiptoeing away from that conversation. Oh, I do remember the time DJ convinced me it was all right to drink saltwater. I thought I was going to die! It's like putting a half cup of salt into a cup full of water and stirring it around until the salt disappears, then drinking it. Gag me with a spoon—gross! Anyway, we will have 400 gallons of water to use and a slow water maker until we dock again, which might not be for weeks.

12:45 P.M.

Here I am on my bunk and out of everyone's way, I can hear the water slapping against the hull as we make our way toward the docks. The faint smell of diesel and oil is seeping into my cabin, making my stomach flip. I wrote some letters to Amy and Laurie again, and then with nothing else to do, I started skimming through my new schoolbooks. I also flipped through the pile of workbooks. Yuck.

My schoolbooks seem to be staring at me. I am dreading the work. I wonder what everyone is doing at school today. I'm in a funk just sitting here, not sure if it is homesick or a little seasickness, or sickness from the fuel and oil smell. I miss HoneyBear and Vicky…everything about being at home. HoneyBear would cuddle with me. She's always there when I feel sad or alone. She would at least lie with me on my bed, nudging me to rub her head and purring to show me she loves me.

2:30 P.M.

NASSAU FUELING DOCK TO PARADISE ISLAND, NASSAU, THE BAHAMAS

This is my time to disappear…hide in my cabin, alone,

and even BabyBear has joined me. She has started roaming around and being curious like a cat. I heard the engine start again and someone jumping onto the deck from pushing off from the dock, which is normal after you untie from the dock. There isn't someone from the dock able or willing to untie and toss the line back to the boat, so most of the time one of us unties and jumps on before we move away. I thought I just heard Dad's upset and angry voice, followed by some loud voices and heavy footsteps. The cabin turned stuffy as the *Western Star* rolled a little from side to side while we backed from the fueling slip. Her engine growled, making me wonder who was growling louder, Dad or the engine. The engine revved louder as Dad or Captain John sped her up, and my cabin door slammed shut. The sound scared BabyBear so much, she jumped straight up. I about fell off the bunk because we were in reverse, and I had nothing to keep me from falling. Not even a grab rail to hold. I caught myself with the edge of the bunk.

This is causing me…well, it's time for some fresh air. Plus, I'm curious about what the commotion was and need to go up on deck to see. The power from the engines is pushing my body back against the wall, making it difficult to move. After peering out of my small porthole—this made me think of how much I miss my house and the large windows. Especially the ones looking out over the barns. This little window, the porthole, is just that—a hole. The boats tied to the dock seem to be skimming past us, but we are the ones moving. My head feels light, I hear more loud voices and heavy footsteps—something isn't right. A few minutes later the splash of the anchor and the chain crashing from the anchor chain compartment in the V-Berth is loud. It's louder than I expected; it's not nearly this loud on deck.

The chain is all out and the clanking is over! All I can hear now is the line connected to the chain as it is pulled out the anchor locker and sent down into the ocean to keep us basically in one spot for the night. I'm in desperate need to go up on deck to get some fresh air so I can avoid getting seasick. Getting seasick simply leaving the dock to anchor out would be embarrassing. Especially since we only moved about 100 yards from the docks, across the inlet. My head is spinning, and the reality of it all is coming together right in front of my eyes. I am about to puke!

Gotta bail!

4:30 P.M.

PARADISE ISLAND, NASSAU, THE BAHAMAS

The loud voices I heard earlier resulted in Bruce leaving the boat! Yes, the tutor! I'm not sure what is going on or what happened, but we no longer have a cook or a teacher. He was a tall man, so maybe he didn't fit in his bunk. Maybe he didn't want to cook. Maybe he didn't get along with Captain John, sharing the V-berth. It seems he really didn't say much...just packed his duffle and left. It looks like DJ and I will be doing a bit more work on deck, and we can handle lines and sails, but who is going to teach me algebra? Maybe we won't have to do any schoolwork. Maybe it's now a long vacation. Sorry. That must have been the diesel and my near seasickness that fogged my thinking, because Mom will not allow that to happen.

After BabyBear scurried quickly from my cabin, I found her hiding in Mom and Dad's cabin. Mom said from now on, she needs to lock BabyBear in the aft cabin while the boat's tied up to the dock, so she doesn't jump off the boat while docked. I guess I can see that, but...

As I looked for BabyBear, I wondered how long it will take her to get her "sea legs" and venture out from the safety of the aft cabin and go up on deck.

Dinner was uneventful but the best part was the pie! We are down to one last pie, and I could only wish to sail back to Bimini for more.

Mom is trying to figure out where everything is in the galley. She wasn't expecting to cook, so the tension in the air is thick. We can feel her mood, and it's not a happy one. Note to self: stay out of her way at dinner and anything she makes, say it's good. I sure don't know how to cook, and I'm not looking for another job to do.

No one confessed to eating the pie. It sure would be great to have one now.

Maybe they will find a pie for DJ's birthday.

Confession—I saw that Mom had saved a little cubed slice out of the last pie for herself. No one saves little bites of food in a baggy like that but her. Maybe this is why the adults are the only ones allowed to open the refrigerator or freezer. So she knows who ate the pie!

We celebrated DJ's birthday with a Bahamian cake and some small gifts. He really wanted to be home and to get his driver's license like all his friends. Today, I felt sorry for him.

SEPTEMBER 22, 1979

Dad and Mom said that today and yesterday have been "regrouping" days. I think they are figuring out how to replace Bruce, mainly because Mom doesn't want to cook or tutor us.

Being anchored out, no one can go to shore and explore. We are stuck here in each other's space, and I mean

DJ is foul today. I'm in my swimsuit but not in the mood to leave my bunk since he is out there somewhere. I miss having my best friends to talk to. Amie and Laurie are the girls I share everything with…everything! We don't go anywhere without each other, unless I am riding and that I do alone—a lot. Laurie, Amie, and I all ride horses and go to the same horse shows together. We love the beach, playing Frisbee, boogie boarding, riding our horses on the beach, or just hanging out. We go to movies, school dances, birthday parties, and on super long trail rides together. Whatever we do, we do it together. People say we are inseparable… or we *were* inseparable. That is…until now. My existence has been turned upside down, inside out, and spun around like a category four hurricane. When it hit land, it hit my reality and shredded it to pieces. I don't like meeting new people, and we left "my people" in California. If only I could go home.

It was only a few months ago that I was at camp with all my friends. We played a massive game of capture the flag. We had all made flour bombs. You just put a scoop of flour in half of a tissue by pulling the two layers apart, then tie them off with little ribbons. They hold together pretty well when tossed, but when you hit something with one of these bombs, it makes a big mess. There was no way of denying you were hit, that's for sure! They also had riding horses, and I learned to ride western and hunt seat and to jump small fences. We sailed little Sunfish sailboats and kayaked across the lake. I learned how to waterski. I was getting good at archery too. The only thing I didn't like was the bonfire. Not the bonfire itself, but when we had to get up on stage and do a skit or something like that in front of all of the campers. It was a couple of weeks of fun and games, until everything changed the moment I got off the bus when I came home.

My mother wasn't at school to greet me, nor was my dad. I was the last one to be picked up. I was sitting on the curb when I saw the little red farm truck pull in, and it wasn't my parents. They didn't drive the farm truck. So, I instantly knew I was being picked up by Mom's new assistant, Fran. She didn't seem to like me or DJ that much. Maybe the feeling was mutual, but anyway, she was hateful. I remember the day she picked me up very well. She spoke with bluntness, informing me that my mom was in the hospital and she wasn't going to tell me why or what had happened. It was the longest twenty-minute drive home. When I saw Dad, he snapped "get in the car," and we were off. Nothing else was said. The worried expression on his face told me everything I thought I needed to know. It was serious, but I didn't know what had happened. A few years ago, Mom had broken her leg falling off of her jumper. She'd flown over the fence, but her horse hadn't. She'd tumbled over the rails of the jump and broken her leg. This was much different, but at the time I couldn't tell. Dad was so upset. The feeling was much like the time I heard about my grandmother passing. And that was nightmarish!

The afternoon's events were life-changing and for me, terrifying. Dad drove to Scripps Hospital, and I remember feeling my heart pounding madly in my chest. He parked, and I followed him at a slow jog up to the automatic doors. We passed the front desk, took the elevator up to the ICU, and walked down the hall to the end room. We were in the ICU...Intensive Care Unit. I held my dad's arm as we entered, and when I saw my mother...that was when I screamed!

The next thing I remembered, I was surrounded by

nurses and then told I couldn't go back in to see my mother unless I calmed down. It was as if I were standing in the dark, both physically and mentally. Seriously, what in the world was going on? My mother lay in the hospital bed looking as white as the sheets on the sterilized bed. She had tubes coming from her nose, her mouth, and her arms. I can still feel the burn from my tears. All I could do was cry and ask, "What is wrong with my mom?" I don't remember too much at the hospital after that. I kind of passed out. I didn't know what was wrong with my mom, but the thing was, the doctors didn't know either. They took her to an operating room for exploratory surgery on her gut and found that her intestines were flipped, and this had caused blood circulation to be cut off, similar to a horse having colic. Since I have seen a couple horses die from colic on the ranch, it made Mom's situation seem much more serious to me. Between her severe allergies to food, medications, and apparently everything in the air in California, and now this…I didn't know what was going to happen. Well, I do know now—we moved onto the *Western Star*.

Back when all this happened, I should have tried to stay busy, hanging out with Amie and Laurie or riding, or I should have taken a trip to the beach. Anything would have helped me escape from what was going on with Mom, but I didn't call my friends or ride much. I felt lost. My mom was the most important person in the world to me, and she almost died. I was sure Amie and Laurie had heard the news about Mom being in the hospital. I was not in the mood for a movie, a ride, or a trip to the beach. I went to the barn and sat with my horses, alone.

I could use a horse's hug right now. I miss them like crazy. I miss the soft touch of a horse's nose, the kissing spot they have between their upper lip and nostrils, and the soft nicker sound Vicky and Dolly make when they hear my footsteps before I even enter the barn, or when they spot me walking down the hill toward them. Mom said she wasn't selling Dolly, that she will be going to Kentucky to retire from showing, so I can trail ride her. I wonder what the trails in Kentucky will be like. I've only ridden in arenas at Crabtree Farms and in the arenas at the horse shows. It will be so cool to ride over the grassy hills of Kentucky.

What the heck was that? A loud thump on the deck, directly above my bunk, felt like something or someone would crash through! I need to check it out.

PARADISE ISLAND, THE BAHAMAS

You won't believe this! The heavy footsteps, the chain rattling above my bunk that scared the tar out of me, was Dad's surprise for DJ and me. Hidden under the two blue canvas covers directly above my bed—they were NOT storage containers—we have two Jet Skis! The noise was Dad and DJ hoisting them off the deck. It was Dad's custom automatic winch, installed specifically for getting the Jet Skis in and out of the water, making all that noise. Hot dog!

We had a quick lesson on how to throttle, stop, and start the Jet Skis and, as Dad was telling us how to get up on them, I slid off the dive platform and sat on the back of my Jet Ski on my knees. I kneeled like that, watching him, until he took one look at me and laughed. Apparently, that's what you do after you start off from your belly, but I'm so little and light, I didn't tip the Jet Ski over. So, I skipped that step! DJ has to start on his belly and pull himself up, a lot like getting up on a surfboard but with a handlebar. He gave it gas, mashed the throttle, made his way to his knees, and then stood up. We learned fast, probably because he can surf and we both ride motorcycles, and riding a Jet Ski is a mix of both. I started mine up and stood, using hardly any throttle at all. I was wobbly at first, but once I gave it a little more gas, I was off and catching up with DJ. Freedom!!!! Dad and Mom gave us wings! It was like galloping off on my ponies, away from everyone. But this time I had to stay near DJ.

We explored the mostly vacant three miles of Paradise Island. There are small canals we maneuvered through, sometimes needing to squeeze through the overgrowth in the tiny inlets, but the challenge was fun, and we both made it through to the other side. We cruised along the mangroves that made up the edge of the island, protecting the beaches and lots of little creatures. We raced along the white sandy beaches when the water was calm. Dad, the history buff, said that the small canals and inlets were made during World War II and used by German submarines for refueling. After the German ships dropped off the fuel, the submarines would slide into these canals and fuel up. It's crazy to think enemy subs were this close to the Florida coast. It didn't look like anyone had been there since the war because the mangroves are so large. Mangroves are home to most fish in The Bahamas, especially baby fish, lobster, and juvenile lemon and nurse sharks. As long as I think "babies," I will be fine! Dad told us all that stuff before we took off on our Jet Skis, knowing the canals were there and that we could ride through them. He's the history guru in the family, not me! But honestly, that was a cool story, especially since we were able to explore the canals and see where the ENEMY submarines fueled! But did he have to tell us what lives in the mangroves!?

The only reason we stopped riding the Jet Skis today

was because we are so tired and hungry. Plus, my feet are pruned! I will be ready for another ride soon. It was amazing. So much fun. It was a little like the freedom I feel when I am off riding on the trails toward Black Mountain. Away from everyone, except for DJ, but I couldn't hear him. I was only "asked" to stay near him.

SEPTEMBER 28, 1979

We have stayed so busy riding the Jet Skis and washing the boat, rolling lines, and other odd jobs like staining teak that sometimes I'm too tired to write. Plus, Mom hasn't forgotten to make sure we are doing some of our schoolwork, so I've been reading at night before I pass out cold. I started reading the *Wilderness Champion* by Joseph Wharton Lippincott, which was given to me by one of my teachers. It was an old library book they were giving away, and she thought I would like it.

SEPTEMBER 30, 1979
PARADISE ISLAND, THE BAHAMAS

We are still anchored out and learning more and more about our jobs and how important it is to take care of everything while living on a boat. It's like taking care of my horse's tack at home. If you don't clean it, wipe it down, and take care of it, it will break. Leather and wood need a lot of care but if you take care of them, they will last a long time. I've had my saddle for years, since I was about six, and it's like brand new, but I was lucky because Anne, our horse trainer, made sure I knew how to clean it and my bridles even when I was just starting out. I had to sell my first saddle because I outgrew it. I hope whoever has it will love it as much as I did.

OCTOBER 1, 1979
NASSAU, THE BAHAMAS

The water here in The Bahamas is so warm. The surface is smooth and clear, unlike the Pacific Ocean. We had sailed down Baja California to Cabo San Lucas a few times a year on the *Sharon Ann*. Speaking of Cabo—I remember the pizza place we walked to from the beach for dinner. Dad made friends with the Italian brothers who owned it. They had a stone oven, apparently like they did in Italy, and the pizzas tasted heavenly. I could eat two pizzas today if we were there!

Cabo's bay was tucked away from the rough waters of the Pacific. The water was calm and clear, transparent-like, clear enough to see the bottom for at least twenty to thirty feet. The white sand covered the long-deserted beach. It was amazing, but the water was always chilly—no, it was cold! A single hotel sat along the beach. It wasn't fancy, but the beach, I am sure, made staying there even more appealing than staying at the other hotels. There was another hotel a short walk down the old street, and they had better food. Mom doesn't like to cook, so we eat out a lot. The beach was so long it would take probably a couple hours to walk down and back, especially if you were looking at seashells. Seldom did we see more than a few people a day. Most of the time, we only saw locals cleaning fish they had caught out in their skiffs. Skiffs are around the size of larger dinghy but not rubber and are used for fishing. In the late afternoon or evenings, when they were done fishing, they would gut the fish right there on the beach. Gross! The fishermen made their money selling their catch to restaurants and people on boats, or traded fish for other supplies. They took the leftover fish home for their own families for dinner. We bought some fish, but Dad's favorite was lobster. He liked to wait for the few locals that would bring in lobster, but either way, he always helped the locals out by buying some of their catch or things that they'd made.

Dad would pull DJ and me behind the dinghy on our surfboards. We had a couple water-ski ropes and would hold on to the rope about ten feet behind the boat, where the wake from the dinghy is the largest. He would pull us up and down the beach for hours. Our dinghy was a small Avon with a little 15-horsepower engine. It had just enough power to keep us up and going. DJ would get some good cuts, turning back and forth across the wake. Sometimes he would jump both wakes in one run, all the way to the other side of the Avon's wake, without falling. Myself, I liked getting up and cruising, crossing the wake a few times, but I could stay up and be dragged behind the boat for as long as Dad would allow it. Surfing behind the dinghy was one of our favorite things to do, but fuel was a pain to go get and this was our ship-to-shore tender. We ran out of fuel for our dinghy on one trip, and Dad had to row us to shore for dinner and back to the boat again. He wasn't in the best mood that day; I think it was hard work rowing a rubber boat with the four of us inside it.

My other favorite thing to do while on the *Sharon Ann* was snorkeling. I would have to wear at least a long-sleeved wetsuit top in the Pacific Ocean, or it would get so cold I would quiver from my head to my flippers. Sometimes it felt like ice water. It seemed like the Pacific Ocean is so much deeper, and maybe that's why it's so much colder than the Atlantic Ocean. In the Pacific, my teeth would rattle and quiver while trying to keep the snorkel mouthpiece sealed in my mouth. It was worth it because snorkeling with the schools of needlefish in that area was totally rad. Needlefish sizes vary from the size of my foot to almost as long as I was tall—well, at ages seven to eleven anyway. I liked following the little needlefish the best. They are surface swimmers like myself, and I would follow them for what seemed to be hours. Staying between the boat and the beach where the water was a little warmer, at least warmer than near the rock cliffs and the arch. I would snorkel until I was too hungry, too cold, or heard the voice of my mom calling me back to the *Sharon Ann*.

Dad and DJ would spend hours scuba diving. They needed to wear full body wetsuits and sometimes used two tanks of air. Once in a while, Dad came back with a fish for dinner. Other times they came back to the boat with stories of seals swimming, bumping, and playing with them. I couldn't imagine a seal playing with me while scuba diving out near the arch—near the open sea. I didn't scuba dive because the tanks were bigger than I was at the time. Or at least that was the reason Dad gave me. Mom didn't because her glasses didn't fit or work inside a mask, and she didn't like it when her ears would get clogged because they wouldn't unclog. We stayed busy, had fun, and I guess in a way, it was getting me ready for this trip. At least the water is warm here in The Bahamas—no wetsuits, no sweaters or jackets. I haven't seen a needlefish yet. I wonder if they live in the Atlantic Ocean?

OCTOBER 2, 1979
LEAVING NASSAU, HEADING TO ELEUTHERA, THE BAHAMAS

Even after exploring Paradise Island together, DJ and

I are still hardly speaking to one another. I think he can't help himself. Privacy is nonexistent on this boat, which seems to be getting smaller by the day. DJ always has to hit me, fart on me, and in this cabin, he loves to slam the door into me while I am trying to get my clothes out for the day. He times it so when I am getting dressed in the little standing room area between the bunks and the door, he opens the door really hard, slamming it into me, and then says real loudly so Mom hears him, "Oh, sorry! I didn't know you were in there." What a spaz! So, if he doesn't want to speak, it's fine by me. I figure not speaking is much better than fighting. Riding off on Vicky is what I would do right now if I were home.

Securing this journal is a bit challenging on deck, but on deck is where I want to be all of the time. The challenge is to keep the journal dry and from flying overboard. Between the wind trying to toss it to the fish in the coral reefs and DJ trying to read it, it's getting a bit frustrating! But everything is frustrating. I feel so angry I could scream.

OCTOBER 3, 1979
SAILING TO ELEUTHERA, THE BAHAMAS

The sails are up and our course and heading are set! Dad is keeping us busy by showing us "the ropes," in more ways than one. That's reaching a little since on a boat a rope is called a line, but even more confusing is when a line is attached to a sail, it's called a sheet. I guess I have started to adjust to our new lives, learning how to do our new chores, when to do our studies, and learning, sometimes the hard way, about the new rules aboard the *Western Star*.

I think about my pony Vicky and my calico cat HoneyBear so much. I wonder if they ever think of me.

Today was my day to secure everything down below deck from the galley to the V-berth. If this job isn't done correctly, something will go flying when we are under sail. Everything on board has its place. Could you imagine your home suddenly being tossed from side to side, up and down, like some ride at the county fair? A glass of water would not only spill but could possibly spill upward and across the room! I could imagine a can of tuna left on the counter in the galley being tossed by a wave. If the can was open…yuck, the smell it would leave with all the little flake bits splashed over the galley and beyond. The only thing I would know to do is find BabyBear. She would clean it up, I bet! Anyway, securing below deck is an important job, but it is one I must do quickly because being down below deck when we begin to move makes me nauseous. Nobody on board knows that I feel seasick while below deck…nor can they find out!

Sailing at six to eight knots is equivalent to riding a cruiser bike down the beach going about seven to nine miles per hour. I decided to sit on the stern of the boat and watch as we leave Nassau. It was fun learning we have Jet Skis and riding them for days exploring Paradise Island.

9:00 A.M.

Beyond the wake of the *Western Star*, Nassau is fading in the distance off our stern. The wind is picking up, and the stronger the wind, the faster our nautical speed. Right now, we are holding a nice sailing speed of eight nautical knots, which to me is when the sailboat is cutting through the ocean, leaning just enough to create a small avalanche of items left out down below. But let the things get tossed—because speed makes sailing exhilarating. Especially sitting on deck, wind slashing my hair around. I think I will move to the bow now before I am asked to go pick up all the things that fell on the floor down below deck.

10:30 A.M.

I had to hold the railing with one hand and my journal with the other because it is windy. Now sitting on the bow, the warm air is hitting my face and continues to whip my hair around. I really need to get some hair bands! What an amazing view. I have never seen so many shades of blue in my life! The sky has a few wisps of clouds and sun rays are dancing across the surface of the ocean and bouncing off the sails and the deck. The *Western Star* must be a sight from off in the distance. However, I can see for miles in all directions, and I don't see a boat or ship anywhere.

12:25 P.M.

Tired of the sun, I moved to the cockpit. Now sitting on the bench seat in the cockpit, next to Captain John at the helm. His job is making sure the autopilot is keeping course while looking out for other boats or debris that might be an issue. The issue would be if we hit something hard floating, like timber or a container lost from a cargo ship, it could sink us! Captain John looks content leaning back in the captain's chair with his arms folded across his chest, looking off into the distance with his dark aviator shades on. He is clean-shaven, his jaw is a white/pink instead of tanned like the rest of his face, and his jet-black hair tosses in the wind. He has old skin, but he's not much older than Dad, I think. What I can't figure out is that Captain John smokes and my mother is extremely allergic to cigarette smoke, and the doctors told her to stay away from all things she's allergic to, plus my father is a licensed captain. So why did he hire Captain John to sail with us? He is very nice and seems to be happy all the time. I have noticed he never smokes in front of or around Mom, and he always has a drink in his hand, in a cup of his own. Dad is down below looking at the nautical charts and maybe doing some last-minute navigation calculations. He usually pops up on deck and has an adjustment for our heading. It's now set, and we are heading to Eleuthera, but there are seven hundred small islands here in The Bahamas. I am sure traveling from point A to point B isn't the straight line people think it should be in an ocean.

It's so cool to be under sail. Small waves are crashing against our bow as the hull slices through the ocean swells. The warm wind is swirling around us and filling the sails, and the seagulls are screeching as they fly above us while begging for a handout. We call them rats with wings because they will eat anything! We aren't allowed to feed them because they will poop on our deck and guess who has to clean the deck—we do. So, we don't encourage them to come near us. They will leave us soon because they like to stay near land. If you see birds feeding from the ocean, it's a sign there are large fish, and so we drop a fishing line off the stern and try our luck at catching dinner.

Just when I was beginning to think Captain John was sleeping because his dark shades hide his eyes and he has been so still, he asked me several questions about the Pacific Ocean and how I like the *Western Star* so far. When he smiles, he doesn't show many teeth, and when he laughs, he laughs with his belly, if he had a belly. He looks strong, and I've seen him fight a sail, a line, and an anchor so far, so I guess he is strong. Captain John told me he's been sailing through The Bahamas most of his life, along with the Caribbean islands, and that The Bahama Islands sit on top of calcium carbonate formations, the stuff that makes seashells. That's why the colors of the water are several shades of turquoise and the other reason why some of the sand on the ocean floor is rock hard. I wonder if these are the only islands built on top of the stuff that makes seashells?

Captain John pointed at each sail and told me the names, then he asked if I knew how to hold our heading… while sailing. He had switched the autopilot off a while ago. He told me the number on the compass to follow, no different than what I did on the *Sharon Ann*. This was my official first time at the helm of the *Western Star*. Totally cool! After I was settled at the helm, Captain John disappeared belowdecks. I felt a little alone and hoped the coral wouldn't pop out of nowhere like the other day. Countless hours I've spent at the helm of the *Sharon Ann*, but that was in the deep Pacific Ocean.

Dad tells people a story about my sailing the *Sharon Ann* all the time—too many times, in my opinion. When I was around eight, on one of our trips sailing down to Cabo San Lucas…as you know, I don't like sleeping in a cabin. Down below is stuffy, and I get nauseous, so I would sit with Dad in the cockpit sometimes all night long. The cold air and salty sprays of the Pacific Ocean would splatter us throughout the night, but I didn't care. I loved being on deck. Anyway, his story goes, "The wind in her sails, the *Sharon Ann* would cut through the Pacific deep swells with her narrow hull like a knife through butter. That night, the moon danced across her white sails while the broken waves sparkled with living organisms and jellyfish. An occasional flying fish hit the deck and sometimes flopped into the cockpit, making us both jump up, grab the fish net, and toss it back. One night, I asked little Annie to take over the helm for a few minutes so I could rest my eyes. I told her the nautical compass heading we should follow for the next few hours, and that is all you have to do. Keep us on course by following the heading, the compass number had to stay on the little line indicating the direction our bow was pointing."

Unlike the *Western Star*, the *Sharon Ann* didn't have autopilot. I was her autopilot on that trip. Dad sat and watched me for a while, but soon he was sound asleep. At night, with or without an autopilot, someone must stay on deck to watch for ships, containers, timber logs, whales, and other items a boat can collide with. These items could easily sink a boat, as Dad has repeated over and over to all of us. As I kept the *Sharon Ann's* setting, the sun was peeking up over the horizon.

His story continues, "I woke up and looked at my watch and looked around the boat."

At the time I wasn't sure what he was looking for besides land. He checked our heading and asked if I'd kept the line on the heading number that he gave me for the whole night. He disappeared down the hatch to the navigational station below and told Mom what he had done.

He continues his story, "After checking the nautical charts, if Annie had held our compass setting, we should see land in about two hours." I had no doubt because I stared into the compass all night and didn't let us move off that heading. He tells the story by adding, "Sharon and I were terrified that we were lost at sea."

But I didn't see it, maybe not at age eight, or because they didn't want me to panic or feel guilty if we were lost at sea. The thought of being lost at sea…they must have been worried out of their minds.

As Dad story goes, "The two hours ticked past as I continued to look for land with my binoculars, praying land would appear. A few minutes later, Land ho!" he says with excitement.

I had no doubt in my mind because again, I had kept us on the exact heading, staring at the compass until my eyes burned. I never let the boat heading deviate, not even the slightest bit. But Dad's story ends, and he tells whoever is listening he was so shocked to see land when we did. Not sure how I feel about him telling that story because I'm sometimes a little uncomfortable with how he tells it. I guess I can be proud of myself for staying up all night and getting us there.

EVENING IN MY BUNK

After Captain John stepped up from the galley, he popped in a tape, and we listened to jazz over the tape-player's stereo speakers. He took the helm, I made my way to the bow of the boat where DJ was hanging out and sat next to him, and we dangled our legs off the bow pulpit, or bowsprit. I held on to the bow pulpit and sat on the bow-sprit! Every once in a while, the bow dipped down, heaved forward, and pitched upward. On the next pitch, our seats lifted off as if we were floating in the air, and then as our butts landed back on the bowsprit's platform, a splash of cool saltwater sprayed us. It was better than a ride at the fair any day! DJ and I laughed together. It was a fun day.

CHAPTER 4

SWAB THE DECK

OCTOBER 5, 1979
ELEUTHERA ISLAND, THE BAHAMAS

We made it to Eleuthera Island—still in The Bahamas. Mom said the name Bahamas comes from the Spanish word "bajamar," which means shallow water. I saw that firsthand as we sailed over it! DJ, Mom, and I sat around the main saloon at the dinette table while Mom read more of her book out loud, and I tried to dive into the chart sitting on the table in front of me.

I couldn't read the chart, listen to Mom, and write, but this is what I did: I measured the distance from one end to the other of Eleuthera Island.

Eleuthera is a long and skinny island. I know how to measure distances on a chart, but turning miles into nautical miles, that takes math. Eleuthera is about 87 nautical miles long and only 1.7 nautical miles wide if measured correctly, so Eleuthera is 100 miles long and 2 miles wide. Measurements are easy to read on a chart because you take the divider tool and there is a scale for nautical miles on the edge of the chart. You put the two ends of the divider so they measure out the distance you want on the scale, and then you take the divider tool and you place one end, in this case the end of the island to start, and then walk it across the island while counting the distance out. But the numbers and lines and all the codes on the charts are what's confusing. I am new at this. I wouldn't want to navigate myself to...well, anywhere! It's hard!

Until Dad comes back to help me with the chart, I will sit and listen to Mom while DJ is working on some schoolwork with his eyes shut on the couch.

Mom continued reading about The Bahamas to us and told me I should read her books when she is finished. My first thought was why not DJ? Shouldn't he be the one to read it? But it would be better if Mom kept reading to us or told us what she read. The stories are interesting, but the books (reading) would probably put me to sleep and definitely would put DJ to sleep. He totally fell asleep while listening to Mom. She continued reading anyway.

The European settlers landed on Eleuthera Island's beaches in 1648 in search of their freedom. I guess that's why they named this island Eleuthera, meaning freedom. They probably landed like we almost did, shipwrecked. Seriously, so far Eleuthera is mangroves, plants, and pretty flat. There is a saltwater lake near the other side (the east side) that I heard is filled with seahorses. I will have to ask Dad if we could go snorkeling there one day.

I spent about an hour listening to Mom read and then when she was finished, I ran to ask Dad about snorkeling with the seahorses. He said maybe, but that has always translated to no.

UP ON DECK

This place is so totally different from anywhere in the Pacific. Catalina Island is a little island off the coast of southern California we sailed to once in a while. It's an island that seemed to pop up out of nowhere in the Pacific Ocean, like a little underground volcano burp, where the Earth had to let go of some extra gas and up popped Catalina Island. We sailed to Catalina several times a year on our first sailboat, which was a 35-foot Ericson. Funny, I remember what type of boat she was, but I can't remember her name. I guess it's because that's what Dad called her—the Ericson. We would sail on the weekends we didn't have a horse show or bike races or one of DJ's racquetball tournaments. I remember now, her name was the *Revolution*, like the song.

Catalina was a full day's sail from San Diego. Leaving before dawn, we would sail up the coast to the LA area and cut over to Catalina. The seas were typically rough and the wind was strong, but the sailing was fast. I would sit up on deck watching Los Angeles as it became smaller and smaller until it vanished behind us. My body would shake from being nervous, or maybe I would be shaking from the cold wind and Pacific Ocean salty spray. DJ and I would watch for porpoise for what seemed like hours. They loved to race the boat and jump into the air like they do at Sea World. When I heard seagulls, I learned that meant we should see Catalina soon. Catalina looked like a small mountain as our little boat sailed near her cliffs. Slowly we could make it to the bay just before the sun sank into the ocean and anchor there.

The next day, we'd take our dinghy to shore and walk up the dock to a little store just off the main street where the end of the dock and beach met. The store reminded me of our small corner store in Rancho Santa Fe. I would ride Vicky there about once a week. With every extra chore done around the house and at the barn, I was given a twenty-five cent allowance over my regular fifty cents per week, and this was much more than some of my friends' allowances. I would use my allowance to buy Jujubes for Vicky and Sugar Babies or a Baby Ruth for me, leaving me with about twenty cents in change I would save for my next ride to the Rancho store. While in Catalina, Mom let me buy one candy—she wasn't a fan of letting us eat sweets. I typically chose Sweet Tarts so they would last longer than a candy bar, and DJ typically chose the Fire Balls. Only a few stores and houses were on Catalina...maybe there were more, but on this side of the island, this is all we saw. Maybe houses were hidden by the trees on the mountain. I don't know because we never explored.

So far, The Bahamas islands look like sandbars with lots of old coral reef stuff, mangrove bushes, and trees, and oh, tons of broken up seashells that got piled up to make an island. I don't know if they were formed from the tides, currents from several channels from all directions, or if from volcanos under the water. I would think they would have more lava rock and be taller if they were made from volcanos under the ocean. The shapes of the islands look like currents raised the sandbars to make the islands. It's possible that the Atlantic Ocean's currents, waves, and winds could have formed these islands and added in the calcium carbonate—the stuff that makes seashells—and many moons ago, palm trees and sea grape shrubs and other tropical plants made their way to these sandbars and these old coral rock islands began to grow and hold them together. Mangroves protect the fish and wildlife, and the coral reefs help protect the land from the ocean waves. As I watched the shoreline, I wondered where the natives are hiding. They must be among the vegetation or maybe inside their small houses, because no one seems to be home.

ANCHORED SOMEWHERE NEAR ELEUTHERA ISLAND, THE BAHAMAS

It's my turn to do the dishes tonight. It's not that bad of a chore, but what chore is great? Doing dishes is like feeding the fish because that's what it is. It is the dishwasher's job to secure all the dishes, including the silverware, into a mesh bag. At the top of the mesh bag is a small line to gather, close, and tie up the opening. Walking up the stairs and back down the ladder to the dive platform is the only challenge of the chore, but most important is the knot tied to secure the bag to the dive platform. If not tied correctly, the dishes sink to the bottom of the ocean. The easiest knot is the bowline, which I learned when I was probably five. I learned a slipknot when I was even younger because that's the knot used when tying horses up. A slipknot is so if a horse gets spooked or anything happens, anyone can pull the long end and the knot slips free, so the horse doesn't hurt itself. Vicky knows how to free herself by pulling on the long end, so I can't leave her tied long. Anyway, I watched the fish feeding frenzy. It was very entertaining, not only to me but to BabyBear as well.

BabyBear knows this is the best time to brave the upper deck because she can see the fish. I watched as she followed me out to the dive platform off the stern. She bounced from the main hatch, to the bench seat, to the aft coach roof, and met me at the dive steps. I was hoping she wouldn't follow me down the ladder to the dive platform, and thankfully she didn't. BabyBear stood watching from above me on deck, staring at the water, as I completed my bowline knot. Make a rabbit hole near the tree, then the rabbit goes out the hole, runs behind the tree, and back into the hole, and pull taut—there is your bowline knot! As the gentle current moved the water, small pieces of food released from the dishes, attracting the colorful reef fish. As they started making their way to the bag one by one, Baby-Bear's eyes widened. Her pupils were dark and black as the fish began to poke their faces into the net. Some kernels of corn floated out of the bag and were snapped up with a small splash, then a bite of hamburger meat disappeared in a flash. They felt the same way I did about canned peas. I saw a fish spit one out as fast as he sucked it in. Mom said that she missed Chino's fresh vegetable stand near our house in Rancho, and I do too. Canned vegetables are nasty.

After about an hour, and a few shakes to the mesh dish bag, pushing it deeper into the water to make sure all the pieces are clean, I took the dish bag back to the galley. There, I untied the knot and rinsed the dishes quickly with fresh water, dried them, and put them away. BabyBear lost interest and went off to explore the upper deck. Mom always has an eye on her while she's on deck, fearful of her falling off the boat. The water is so calm, I'm guessing because we are surrounded by miles and miles of sandbars. The sun disappeared a while ago, and stars fill the sky, so I'm on deck. It's too dark to keep writing, but I can see the glow of Captain John's cigarette on the aft deck.

After Captain John took the last draw of his cigarette, he joined me on the bow looking up at the sparkling sky. He pointed out the constellation Cassiopeia. I wasn't familiar with it, but I showed him Orion's belt and shared the story of how my grandmother and I have matching

Orion's belt freckles on our upper forearms. The Big Dipper, he says, was also called the saucepan. I've never heard that before, so I'm not sure if he is telling me the truth or not. Then he showed me how to locate the North Star, how it lies between the Big Dipper and the constellation Cassiopeia. He said the North Star is the most important star in the sky for navigating boats. North is actually short for Northern Hemisphere. The North Star will be the same, and in the same location all of the time. It will angle above the horizon as your latitude. He said he would show me how to measure this with our sextant one day. I will have to see this to understand it more, but I have seen Dad use the sextant several times. After our star gazing, he wondered off, so I'm going to grab a blanket and pillow and spend the night under the blanket of stars—in the fresh air—without DJ!

OCTOBER 10, 1979
CRUISING ELEUTHERA

Today, DJ and I went on the Jet Skis and rode alongside the *Western Star* while she was under motor-sail. We were not allowed to cross the bow, but we jumped the little wake behind the boat, cruised closer to shore, and raced. Holding the throttle steady was so much easier today, and falling off was too. I was a little nervous waiting for the ski to circle back—it seemed like it was moving in slow motion as my mind wandered to what creatures were lurking beneath my dangling legs. I didn't dare look. I will try harder not to fall off next time, but really, what's the fun in that? The water is clean, clear, and warm—cooler than bath water but the only shivering from me would be from nerves. I could feel a fish brush up against my skin and suddenly its little wake pushed against me as it scurried off. I grabbed the Jet Ski, wiggled my way up on the deck, and rode off. When I got tired of standing, I plopped down to my knees and rode in that position for a while. But when standing, I could see straight down to the bottom, to the ocean floor. I scared a few fish, parted a few schools of fish, and saw lots of conch sitting on the sandy floor. It was hard to tell if I was in ten feet of water or thirty. Mom waved her arms signaling for us to come back to the *Western Star*, and as I slowed down, I heard the sonar beeping while Dad and Captain John set the anchor.

We tied the Jet Skis to the stern and boarded. My legs felt like a Jell-O mush—strawberry Jell-O mush, because of the red color of my skin. We must have ridden for two hours at least. Mom tossed DJ and me some shampoo and soap—her way of saying it was bath time. DJ and I sat on the dive platform and suds up—I shampooed and swirled my long, tangled hair on top of my head, finished washing, and jumped back into the water. I had to do about five summersaults floating away from the stern of the boat before the suds would rinse out of my hair. Then I rested, floating on my back and listening to the ocean sounds. It wasn't like the Pacific Ocean. Snorkeling in the Pacific, I could hear the waves crashing in the distance. Here it's more the slight movement, maybe movement of little living things or fish, an echoing sound, a high-pitched sound maybe, but not the sound of a boat's engine or a sailboat. I'm just not sure what I was hearing, but I felt weightless and free resting on the ocean's surface. After a couple minutes, I heard Mom yelling my name and looked up at her. I had floated a couple boat lengths away and my legs were tired, so I made my way back with my arms only, doing the breaststroke. Saltwater is great. I can float for hours without any kind of life jacket. Part of me wants to float all the way back to California and part of me wants to stay. I guess next time I will hold onto a line or the dive platform when I am this tired, unless I want to float back to the US.

My bed feels so comfortable, and my pillow is nice and cool. I think I'll rest my eyes for a minute. Maybe I will write a letter…

Sometimes it takes me days to find a place to write without prying eyes, or when I sit it must look like I am not doing anything, so I am given a task or a job to do, and it's always followed by: and do some schoolwork when you are done!

OCTOBER 12, 1979

What "appeared" on deck this morning was our masks, snorkels, and fins! DJ and Dad were getting their masks on, and I was right behind them.

The water felt like cool bath water as I cleared my mask, adjusted my snorkel, and followed the sounds of my dad and brother. Sand carpeted the ocean floor below the *Western Star*, and as I looked forward a bit, I noticed Dad and DJ free diving, following the hull down to the keel. They seemed to be inspecting it, along with the sonar and depth finders. Dad took a pass around the prop (propeller), and I watched the large fish as the large fish watched them. I followed them from above and snorkeled around to the bow of the boat and watched as they stopped at the anchor line. They gave the "okay" sign—diving and snorkeling are cool because the dive sign language is used to communicate. You can always see what the others are saying without having to be close to hear them. The "okay" sign was followed by the "going down" sign. They swam down along the anchor line to the long chain and followed it until they saw the anchor resting on the sand. It didn't seem to be doing much, but we were not moving either. They signaled the "going up" sign and joined me on the surface.

We swam around while waiting for Mom to finally join us. When she arrived, Dad signed the "follow me" sign, so DJ and I followed him like little guppies with Mom right behind us. It wasn't much of a swim, as my arms were at my sides feeling weightless; smooth, forceful kicks with my fins allowed me to glide through the water with ease. DJ would try and kick me in the face with his big fins once in a while, but I was lucky enough to dodge those big stinky things. We snorkeled over seagrass and saw a few seahorses. I've always wanted to see a seahorse in the wild. Poor little dudes have to flutter around with those useless fins and grab onto the seagrass to stop themselves from drifting away. As we reached the rocky area, Dad pointed out some fire worms peeking out of the crevices they call home. We reached a coral reef that was totally cool. The oranges, purples, greens, and reds of the coral, sea fans, and sea rods were so bright. The colors reminded me of the paintings on the restaurant walls in Bimini. A cute little yellow tang darted around, while the swirly colors of yellow, white, black, and blue on the angelfish caught my attention. The angelfish swam slowly, almost at a standstill, as I passed… she was staring right back at me. The sea anemones swayed from side to side with their tentacles dancing like arms above their head, waving or swaying to some music. A little orange, white, and black striped clown fish darted in and out of his home while staring excitedly at me. Dad had to nudge me to get my attention, and then he cupped his hands together—the sign for us to go back to the boat.

My lips are pruned…my hands, my feet. I am one big <u>pruny</u> pink and brown raisin!

Dad told us at dinner that this island is known for nurse sharks, especially in June and July, but he repeated, "They won't hurt you." Why don't I feel reassured?

ELEUTHERA ISLAND, THE BAHAMAS

We have sailed short distances down Eleuthera Island almost every other day. The 110 miles seem more like 510. The annoying beeping from the sonar was making me crazy, but seeing right to the bottom of the ocean floor with our bare eyes makes for a cool and excellent ride. DJ and I have been hanging out—kind of hanging off—the pulpit, spotting and counting tropical fish swimming below us, including stingrays and some sharks. Dad assured me they were harmless as long as there wasn't blood in the water, nor should we splash around.

The bowsprit is our favorite hangout. DJ and I wear our headsets blasting tunes from our Walkmans. It helps soften the annoying beeps and the chaos coming from the adults in the cockpit because the charts are wrong and the channels were moved after the hurricane. My go-to cassette tapes are Supertramp, the *Long Way Home*; Queen's *Bohemian Rhapsody*; Journey; Styx; Simon and Garfunkel; and totally Aerosmith's *Walking in the Sand*, plus a few more like Blondie, Tom Petty, and Fleetwood Mac. DJ loves Guns N' Roses, Van Halen, ZZ Top, Kiss, Cheap Trick, Foreigner, and the Rolling Stones. In eighth grade, a friend of his from Rancho Santa Fe School had Van Halen play at his house for his birthday. This was right before their album became big. That was so cool, and I wish I had been old enough to have gone. Mom listens to Linda Ronstadt,

ABBA, Barbara Streisand, Rita Coolidge, Neil Diamond, and anything Elvis. She's a huge Elvis fan, and even took me to an Elvis concert. I think I was about two and she couldn't find someone to watch me, so she took me with her. She tells that story a lot. We are lucky we have these new Walkmans and a cassette tape player in the cockpit. I think we would have gone crazy without music.

Music is huge in The Bahamas too. At that fun restaurant with the great pies, I read a little thing that said the islands of The Bahamas were nicknamed "the Islands of Song." The art hung around the little plaque was several music-themed paintings. Some were of music horns, silhouette dancers holding instruments, instruments of all types, a guitar being played in the shade of a palm tree, and several shapes and sizes of drums. In one of the paintings, it looked like pots and pans were being used as instruments. Maybe they were drums that looked like pots and pans, I am not sure. The paintings made me notice the tunes playing in the restaurant. It was island music! It had a fun dancing beat and groove with lots of drum sounds; maybe those are the steel drums—it was cool. It was like a party in a song—if that makes sense.

SAILING NEAR ELEUTHERA, THE BAHAMAS

As we make our way down Eleuthera, sailing and watching the fish below, I spend a lot of time helping Captain John reroll lines and mop the deck. DJ and I do like turning into pirates while we swab the deck, until it turns into a face full of soap. Those *drasted* mop-weapons have stinging bubbles on their ends. One should walk the plank after swabbing someone's face. We drop anchor and jump in the water immediately to swim around. I'm learning how to free dive. At first, I couldn't figure out why we had to "learn" to free dive, but soon I found out that swimming deep down into the ocean is a little different than swimming down to the bottom of a pool. Buoyancy is my number one obstacle. The first five feet are hard unless you dive in from the boat, but then your mask and snorkel bash your face or fall off. My fins help, but sometimes it takes a little more effort to get past the first five. After that, the weight of the water stops pushing me upward. Past about the five-foot mark, then the trick is knowing how much longer I can hold my breath. Dad made it down to the ocean floor (about fifteen to twenty feet, I think) a few times and brought huge conch shells up. Later we ate them for dinner—not the shell, the conch. Again, I laugh at my own jokes, even when they aren't funny.

SALOON, DINETTE TABLE

As I was sitting at the table writing, Dad challenged me, and I am totally digging it. I will try and write some notes in my journal to help me remember. He is teaching me to read and learn to navigate using the nautical charts, reference charts, parallel ruler, or a plotter and dividers. All of these fun-looking tools. I love challenges!

I am trying to remember, but I truly believe that after he started, I was so confused I would have sailed us straight to China if we used my calculations. The four basic concepts of navigation are position, direction, distance, and the sea depth. It started off simple, anyway. He's back… here we go again. Time to focus!

Dad said for me to think of a pole running through the globe from north to south for the positioning of the latitude and longitude lines. I've got this…the latitude lines are the make-believe lines wrapping up and down (north to south) on the globe. Longitude runs with the equator—wrapping around Earth like a belt. Wait, do I have that backward? Ugggh.

I am confused!

Mom came in and joined us in the saloon where Dad was trying to show me something on the chart, and she started reading about The Bahamas. I am completely lost trying to listen to two things at once, but DJ seems completely oblivious to everything.

OCTOBER 19, 1979

Everyone seems to fade in and out of spaces aboard the *Western Star*. It's not like in a house when you enter or leave a room with a purpose. It's hard to explain, but we enter spaces on the boat sometimes without a reason, maybe because of the lack of space, and if you take two steps you have entered another living area—a space someone is occupying—there are no boundaries and no rules unless a door is shut. Even then it's not the occupant's space for long.

OCTOBER 30, 1979

Maybe if I write this chart stuff down, I will remember it. Or maybe not!

Wait. LONGitude is up and down—long things hanging from the top of the Earth! LATitude is like a belt. I have to think of something to help me remember and not get them mixed up again.

The equator is always 0 degrees. The angle of longitude is measured… I've already forgotten the rest. Oh, yes, lines of latitude and longitude are measured angles formed from the center of the Earth in degrees and minutes and tenths of minutes (fractions—dang it) and there are 60 minutes in 1 degree; a circle has 360 degrees. This actually might be correct, but it doesn't really explain reading a chart. My eyes are glazing over as I try and write this down. I need a break. I'm going topside!

TOPSIDE, NEAR PULPIT

My head is foggy with charts, and I can't stop thinking about home.

When I walk outside of our house in Rancho, I walk down the hill always wearing my boots because of snakes, but now when I walk outside, I am still on the boat, making me feel stuck or trapped. I wonder if this is how my horses feel when they are left in a stall? I wish we had a television. I wish I was Samantha on *Bewitched*. I could wiggle my nose and poof, there's a TV! Better yet, wiggle, wiggle, and poof, and I would be back in California.

ON MY BUNK

So…I am determined to at least understand nautical charts. And if that means I have to write down some of the meanings or tricks, I will! So, here goes: A nautical mile is one minute of latitude. I have no idea what that means, but that is a fact. I just want to use the parallel ruler thing and know what to do. I did read about all the little symbols used for warnings, obstacles, and danger in the water. The little + and * signs on the blue (water) part of the charts are where hazards are located! And you're supposed to stay in the middle of the red and green markers lined up going into a harbor. Yep, you guessed it. I already knew that from being on the *Sharon Ann*, but I never noticed them on the chart before, so that's something! Dad always said to remember, "Red Right Return," which means keep the red buoys on the right of the boat when returning to land. Now for some new stuff. Shazbot!

If it were up to me to chart our course, we would need to learn a new language, like Chinese. Thankfully, I am not in charge of chart reading or finding our headings. I hope I can remember all the information Dad has told me for the next lesson. If there is a next lesson. If Dad still has the patience to teach me, I would be willing to try.

NOVEMBER 1979
CAPE ELEUTHERA PENINSULA
HEADED TO COORDINATES: 24.836543, -76.343311

We start to sail carefully around the peninsula of Cape Eleuthera, and the winds have gone from slight to fierce, quickly. We drop the sails as we near the canal entrance to the yacht club. The wind pushed the *Western Star's* fifty-three-foot hull sideways like it was a toy. Out here, we are at the mercy of Mother Nature and She just proved to us She is in charge.

The engine grumbled and growled, and we were pushed so far off course, Dad slammed her into reverse and at full force drove her backward, away from the rocky shore. From the deck, I could hear the rattling of the cabinet and drawers from the vibration of the engines. The entrance seemed to move from being straight ahead of us to twenty feet to the right in a second. Hearts were thumping—at least mine was! All hands on deck to help in any way needed. I was yelled at to put my life vest on because the wind was so strong and they knew it wouldn't take much more to blow me off the boat. Dad started heading toward the entrance again, this time at least twenty feet to the right of the canal entrance, and as we made our way forward, we were right in line with the canal. The wind continued howling and pushed us away from the docks toward the coral breakwater wall. As we entered the yacht club marina, we were spun a quarter of the way around. At this point, we could have hit a huge yacht or the coral breakwater wall, and either way didn't look good. As Dad pushed the engines to a mere scream, louder and louder it grumbled. We were fighting the wind to get the *Western Star* closer to the dock. Captain John tossed a line to someone on the fuel dock. Two men grabbed the first line, securing it to a huge cleat attached to the dock. Then Captain John used the electric winch to pull us in as DJ threw another line to the dock from our stern and cleated the line off. A third line was secured and, between the engines and winches working together, we slowly pulled close enough to the dock to feel relieved that we didn't hit one of the fancy yachts or crash up on the wall. I have never seen wind that strong come up that fast. That was terrifying.

CAPE ELEUTHERA MARINA & YACHT CLUB, THE BAHAMAS

At every port, Dad finds a phone to call my granny and let her know we are alive and well. She's so worried about us exploring and sailing around on a sailboat. She envisions pirates, hurricanes, and sinking ships. Dad promised her we would each have our own emergency beacon, and we do. They are secured to the wall next to the steps at the main hatch with our names written on each one to identify which one belongs to whom. At least if the ship goes down, we would have a chance at someone finding us floating in the deep blue. Dad gave us a "safety course" before leaving Bimini too, telling us about our personal emergency beacons, EPIRBs. Each one is registered with our names and information, and we are to grab our EPIRB in case of an emergency, LIKE if the boat is sinking! When it's turned on, it alerts search-and-rescue and other boats in the area of a man-overboard distress signal, but it only lasts a day or two. I don't want to think of what happens after that nor should Granny know!

On Dad's call to Granny from Bimini, I overheard him explaining that we "park" at big floating parking lots in the ocean at night so we can sleep. I thought to myself, these must be floating docks with gas stations and a market too. He lied to her, so she could rest at night and not worry so much. If she only knew we were out, under sail, in all sorts of weather and conditions in the dark of night, she would be truly beside herself. I am glad she didn't hear about our crazy arrival here yesterday. At least the storm passed, or the worst of it did, anyway. The wind is still strong, but we are safe. This morning we moved into a boat slip away from the fueling dock. The *Western Star* has a "hotel room" where we can all sleep without worry.

NOVEMBER 8, 1979

Our fresh bread is gone, fruits and milk...anything that isn't in a can, has been eaten. We have lots of canned and frozen food, but no one wants to eat a tuna fish sandwich without bread, and the bread in The Bahamas is the best bread I have ever eaten! We caught a grouper yesterday and ate it for dinner. It was good, better than something canned or frozen. In the Pacific Ocean once in a while, we would drag a fishing line behind the *Sharon Ann*. Sometimes we would catch a tuna, but that's not the same tuna as tuna in a can. It was a challenge to reel a large fish in and onto a sailboat, but Dad would try. When successful, he would fillet the fish—most of the time it was a tuna—right off the stern. It was gross! He dipped and cleaned the fillets with ocean water, and we would have the best fresh sushi ever. Mom always waited to have hers cooked. It took me awhile to brave my first taste of sushi. No sushi last night, though! We grilled the big grouper after we hauled him up from about fifty or sixty feet below our hull.

NOVEMBER 12, 1979

Everyone has fun going to shore! At every marina or yacht club, we find different and new places to explore. Sometimes the locals have coconuts for sale. They chop the top off with one quick slice using a machete. I love to drink coconut milk fresh after they chop the top off. Then you hand the coconut back, and a couple more chops help peel the coconut meat out easier. It always amazes me how well they can use a machete. I can imagine tonight's dream—I wake up screaming. On the dark beach, I ask the stranger to chop my coconut, and then I start to notice warm liquid running down the side of my body. When I look down at my left hand, it's no longer there…my whole arm is gone. Oh, my! No more thoughts of machetes. I just gave myself the willies!

NOVEMBER 15, 1979

DJ and I can't wait to go to the store. Maybe we can get a candy bar? DJ simply wants to get off the boat. I think Mom "wins" for being the most excited to get off the boat, at least for a little while, for sure! She practically dragged us off the boat, and she is one of the slowest people I know. No offense, Mom. Thank goodness she's never going to read this.

NOVEMBER 25, 1979

The yacht in the slip next to us is almost double the size of the *Western Star*. It's a huge, brand-new motor yacht named the *Monkey Business*. She flies the American flag and is from Aventura, Florida—it says it in paint along with her name on her hull's stern. She's probably eighty or ninety feet long. Okay, not double the length of the *Western Star*, but she must be at least three *Western Stars* as far as the interior decks. She has three tiers of floors and decks, including the upper deck and outside decks. I don't know the names of these decks, but I say it how I see it! The lower, open deck area is on the stern and used to get to the dive platform and to fish from. There are heavy-duty fishing rods, a comfortable-looking fighting chair, and built-in coolers. The middle deck has lounge chairs, and the upper top deck has a Boston Whaler dinghy mounted—somehow—way up there. The bridge where the captain mans the helm is up on the top deck as well. I bet they have a cook and maybe a housekeeper too. I wouldn't want to run out of fuel or have engine problems on her. She has no sails!

10:00 A.M.

The yacht club rents golf carts! Mom rented one, and DJ drove us to the store. It wasn't much of a store, but I will call it that. Mom complained about the prices and the poor selection of things, but we bought groceries. They had the basics like bread and milk. DJ drove the golf cart back to the yacht club. Needless to say, I held on extra tight—I was terrified even though he is driving age. Every time he thought I wasn't paying attention or holding on, he would zigzag sharply to try and toss me from the golf cart. He's such a dork!

CHAPTER 5

MONKEY BUSINESS

NOVEMBER 26, 1979

CAPE ELEUTHRA MARINA

24.836543, -76.343311

Did I tell you Dad doesn't meet a stranger? I guess while at the fuel dock fueling and filling up our water tank, he's made friends with the people on the *Monkey Business*. How does he do that—make friends with strangers—and so fast? I have to admit it would be super cool to check out the inside of that huge boat!

Wow, can you say embarrassing! Not cool! My stomach is twisting and doing somersaults like an Olympic gymnast. Dad has set up a "playdate" for me with the girl on board the *Monkey Business*. I guess they are going out for a short cruise and somehow, I was invited. I am way too old for my parents to set up a "playdate." I don't want to go! It's so hard to talk to strangers. Mom says I am painfully shy. I am not sure if she means it is painful for her or for me. I mean, it is not fun for me even thinking about being around new people. And did I say I will be alone? I have no idea what to say, or what to talk about, or what to do. BUT it would be totally cool to see inside that huge yacht.

I do miss my friends, so making a new friend might be nice. I don't know. BabyBear has been my only "friend" for several weeks now, and I am good with that.

I hear Dad calling me. It looks like I don't have a choice. I'm going.

8:00 P.M.

Jackie seemed as shy as I felt. It wasn't an instant "best-friend" experience, but she was nice and wanted to show me her stateroom. Stateroom! I have to share a small cabin with DJ, and she has a huge stateroom all to herself. I decided it would be cool to see it, though. From the dock, we stepped up on a small ramp with a tall wire railing located on the starboard side. The ramp led up to a glass door, and we entered on the mid deck of the yacht. We walked into the saloon that had a fancy bar area with mirrors and fancy-looking bottles and glasses hanging from the ceiling and walls. This made me wonder how they keep them from crashing to the floor while at sea. I stepped into the entry way and felt cool air—air conditioning. It was awesome! I stood under the vent and let the cold air flow over my face. The air swirled my hair around, and I didn't want to move. If I were a sea anemone, my hair would have been standing straight up and dancing in celebration. I noticed that all of the chairs and sofas were covered in fancy white leather, and the carpet was soft and fluffy. Nothing like the floors on the *Western Star*. There were huge windows in every direction around the room. Everything was amazing—beautiful, new, and spotless.

For a second, I felt guilty that DJ didn't get to come and check this out, but only for a second. I felt bad, but really, I needed to get away from DJ. It's not enough being on the other side of the boat. I swear I can smell him from anywhere.

Jackie led me down some steps to another floor that ended in a large hall with reddish color wood, not the typical teak like most sailboats. The doors were sturdy, not thin like the *Western Star's* doors, and the doorknob was round like doorknobs at home. Jackie led me into her cabin—her stateroom—on the port side, and then she dragged a container from under her huge bed and we sat on the lush carpet floor. Instantly, I felt the vibration and heard the engines get louder. Footsteps on the deck, followed by a line being tossed onto the deck, making the familiar slapping sound, and then the yacht began to move backward. I panicked at first. A rush of fear ran through me, and my face probably turned a few shades of red. I wanted to bolt for the deck, but the boat was so big that I didn't know where any of the decks were. Jackie poked my arm and asked me what I wanted to play. The container was filled with toys, so I checked them out. The feeling of the boat spinning caught my attention once again, and then the engines thrust the boat forward. My mind went back to the toys. I didn't think of it again, at least not for a while.

The air-conditioning seemed to cure my need to flee to the top deck. I had no motion sickness; not even the slightest feeling of green gills came over me. I was so thankful and really wish we had air-conditioning like that on the *Western Star*! Jackie and I played for about an hour before she disappeared into the head. After a long while,

I decided to go to the only area I had seen prior to the stateroom—the saloon. I went up the steps and entered the saloon. Several adults stared and made me feel out of place. Well, I was.

Why did Dad send me?

I looked around and couldn't find Jackie anywhere. I started to feel the ocean's swells and held on to the counter of the bar so I wouldn't land on someone's lap. I watched and wondered how the glasses and drink bottles were staying stationary. It seemed they stayed with the help of beautiful stainless steel racks, or holders, that cradled each bottle and glass. That was slick. On the *Western Star*, we have to wipe and polish anything stainless-steel almost every day or it will start to tarnish and turn dull. My parents don't drink at all, not even an occasional glass of wine, so something like this wouldn't be on the *Western Star*. I felt the bow dip and rise, again and again. Unlike a sailboat, the motor yacht hits the top of the swells, smacking them and causing a jolt like I've never felt before. My legs vibrated and then my whole body. Her bow dipped downward, then started to rise up, lurching forward and upward owing to the power of her engines. A sudden but slight falling sensation caused my whole body to be slightly airborne, and then suddenly her hull whacked the top of a swell once again. This caused a slight quake throughout the yacht. The larger the swells grew, the harder her hull shuttered after every hit. It wasn't a pleasant motion and it seemed everyone disappeared, so I jumped onto one of the sofas. For the rest of the trip, I watched the swells approach the yacht. They looked at least five to six feet but felt larger. Maybe since I was way up high on the second-story deck, the swells looked smaller, I don't know. They sure felt bigger than six-foot swells. When I looked out at the sea and watched the swells from their yacht, it seemed to help with the motion sickness because thank goodness, I didn't get sick. The cold air conditioner, and how hard it blew around the cabin, was my favorite thing about my trip. I am sure it helped me from actually becoming ill. I did pretend I was on a crazy ride at the fair, and that seemed to help keep my mind off getting queasy too. But I still wonder why the captain didn't take us back to the docks sooner.

Dag, we were out at sea for hours in that mess. But we made it back to the dock, and I am able to write about it!

Jackie was really embarrassed that she had gotten so incredibly seasick. It didn't bother me, but I am so very glad to be back home. Yes, home…on the *Western Star*.

CHAPTER 6

THE SPINNAKER RIDE

DECEMBER 3, 1979

SAILING: ELEUTHERA TO LITTLE SAN SALVADOR, THE BAHAMAS

My hair whipped around like a lasso above my head as I ran, skipped, and hopped across the slanted deck chasing after my favorite hat that now has vanished in the deep—dark—ocean—blue. The sails are up and secured, but my hat—not so much. I took one more lap around the deck to secure everything, walking at a tilted angle while holding on as the bow dipped and lurched, up and down. The *Western Star's* hull is at a slanted tilt with the horizon, which is the heel rotation on a boat. Timing is everything in big seas for walking on deck or in the cabin. Move on the high side of the roll, which means walk faster while the bow starts its rise going upward. Slow and hold tight in the fall. It becomes a pattern, but the larger the waves, the more challenging it is to move. There are so many lines and rigging wires throughout the boat, it's fairly easy to find something to hold onto. It's even a challenge to move five feet and can be awfully hard in large ocean swells—waves that haven't crested. The faint sound of music coming from the stereo system is overtaken by the hull cutting through the ocean's swells, so ends up sounding like someone doing a huge cannonball off a high dive at the pool. Even wind filling the sails is a swooshy, flapping sound. The sails seem to be talking or giving hints to Dad for what's to come.

I've learned not to sail the *Western Star*, but to help her sail! I love that saying! Everyone seems to naturally know to sit on the upward side of a sailboat. I guess if you sit on the low side, it's like leaning back in a recliner chair without a head rest to support your head. DJ and I pretend to be hiking out, like we've seen people doing on the sailboat racers. They sometimes stand on the edge of the hull to keep from tipping over. We leaned way back against the high-side railings, until a couple huge waves crashed over our bow and completely soaked both of us. The cold water made us jump, and we both ran for a dry sun spot on deck to get warm. It's the fun little moments with DJ that make me not want to toss him over. Although he's so much stronger than I am, I know who would end up overboard. Yes—yours truly.

3:20 P.M.

The *Western Star* is cutting through these really big swells, making way like a champion, and it's time to listen to a little Queen. I pushed play on my Walkman and "We Are the Champions" is playing. I've tucked myself, along with my journal, on deck near the Jet Skis, and I'm jamming. I use one Jet Ski as an anchor to keeping me from sliding down to the port side and probably off the boat. The deep dark turquoise blue ocean was becoming darker like the Pacific as we sailed along into deeper seas. The color seemed to put me in some kind of a trance. The sea seemed untamed, like a wild horse trying to buck someone off its back. Each swell must be about five to six feet or more. It's hard to sit out here and concentrate on anything other than what Mother Nature has given us today.

When sailing, it keeps sailors looking up. These swells are tiring my legs from balancing on the Jet Ski, and I am sitting down. A grumbling feeling takes over—I'm hungry. It seems I haven't eaten all day and typically, on a boat, we seem to munch on crackers or chips…or anything available all day long. I haven't had anything to eat. I wish I had a pie.

5:00 P.M.

There seems to be no way to describe walking on a sailboat in six- to eight-foot seas, or in any seas, and under sail. Maybe it's like…walking on a moving kiddy roller-coaster ride at a fair that is always in a tight turn. I will keep trying until I figure out how to best describe it. But the fact is, one wrong move while walking and you could be swimming, cut yourself on a cleat, trip over a line, hit your head on the boom, or catch a line across the body or neck.

I cautiously made my way below deck, holding onto the grab rails. When I passed DJ, he asked me to make him a tuna sandwich. The first steps down the hatch, I felt my feet sink down into each step of the ladder, the next two were practically airborne, and the last a hard hit heave. The boat's pitch was increasing, or maybe it felt like we were "tipping" farther because I was below deck. A pain shot through my hands as I slapped them around the ladder, catching myself before falling. My hands are still red. As I faced the galley and reached for the counter, I was suddenly airborne, and then when the floor reached back up to my feet, my knees buckled. I regained control by becoming one with the cupboards in the galley, bracing myself up against them, and then timed the waves so I wouldn't be bruised by slamming into them on the downward thrust. Challenge taken, this became a game to conquer the bucking bronco while standing up. I felt the rhythm of the waves and anticipated the next, like I was riding her deck, but unfortunately it was like riding a wild horse, and they have no mercy on the rider.

Opening each cupboard and drawer created a new challenge. The challenge was to not let everything fly out! The only thing I could do quickly was grab some crackers, but I managed to get two slices of bread and a can of tuna for DJ. Placing the can of tuna in the middle of the slices, I wrapped it with a paper towel and handed it up to him through the hatch. It took him a minute to realize what I had done. I could imagine how proud he looked when he thought he had forced me to make him a sandwich. One second later, his voice rang out, "Doofus," but I'd made my point. He understood that he had to make his own sandwich.

To avoid his wrath, I walked through the little hall to the aft cabin to make sure BabyBear was okay. In the stern, there isn't as much motion, nor as much of the up and downward slamming like midship or in the bow. Most of the harsh movements are felt in the bow! In the stern or in the aft cabin, the movements are felt but not so drastic. The aft head's porthole has a layer of thick salt as the ocean continues spraying it every pitch, roll, heave, and sway we take. The couple tacks we have done caused all of the things not secured to fall down to the middle of the aft cabin's floor. Even the mattress from the smaller bunk had slid off and was half covering the supplies not secured. The cabin looked as if it had been tossed like a salad, with paper towels, toilet paper, bags of chips, large bulk packages of crackers and other nonperishable foods, and a mattress on top. The head door was locked open with a little hook latched to the wall, clanging every few seconds. BabyBear was curled up in the sink in the aft head, safely away from any flying objects. She seemed unscathed from the wreckage in the aft cabin. Those are Mom's words, not mine. Mom has jammed herself in a corner of her bunk and is reading a book. BabyBear greeted me with a soft little mew. I heard her motor start as I softly scratched her chin. Mom knew I was hiding from DJ but didn't seem to mind and continued to read. As I left, she lifted her head from her book and said, "You need to start on your science book now." As much as the thought of schoolwork was like hearing fingernails run down a chalkboard, I remembered there was a chapter on clouds, and today I think I saw every cloud shape in the sky!

6:44 P.M.

I went back through the galley to the saloon, grabbed the book, and headed back up on deck. This time I stayed in the cockpit to enjoy a cushioned seat and a backrest. I sat on the leeside, sheltered from the wind. I'm on the side closest to the water because of the boat leaning from all the wind in the sails. I could almost touch the ocean if I sat near the railing and reached off the side. The spray from the ocean hit me almost every couple seconds, but it felt nice. I could rest the book on my legs, and it was as if

I were in a recliner, leaning back, but a comfortable chair at home wouldn't be beating on my back or tossing me up in the air every couple seconds. As I found the chapter on clouds, DJ appeared from below deck and said, "Totally rad idea. I should go get my schoolbooks and hope they fall overboard too." He's hardly looked at any of his books since we arrived. He probably doesn't know where they are! It wouldn't shock me if he had tossed them overboard already.

DECEMBER 4, 1979

Growing up on the water, I've learned instinctively how to read the clouds and, personally, if my hair starts to curl up, rain is about to come! My hair is 100 percent accurate. The clouds give weather warnings to sailors and can save lives. Some old sayings are even worth remembering, like "Red sky at night, sailor's delight. Red sky in the morning, sailors take warning." However, reading about the clouds and weather in my schoolbook is a bit dull. Well, it just makes something I already know confusing. Makes me wonder if I had it all wrong. The book only gives the names and the definitions. It would be easier to read a story of a cloud. Wouldn't it be cool to read about a baby cloud growing up to be a huge cumulus and all the shapes it takes on for the people below to have fun guessing the animals within it, and the jokester cloud, the nimbus, chasing around people with its rain. I know that wouldn't be in a textbook, but it sounded fun.

MY CLOUD STORY:

A parade has started above our heads. One by one they formed in clusters that grew quite some time ago. Now, dozens drift about. The fluffy and dense, white cotton cumulus reach toward one another as they march on. Mother Nature has started painting on her blue canvas we call the sky. Her paint brush adds white wisps, a light stroke here and there and everywhere. It's her masterpiece, the cirrus, light as a curl of hair. Over the seas far, far away, the cumulonimbus gathers his strength and grows to billowing heights. His muscular stature and his flat, dark bottom slash at the sea and land. He dumps out black thin lines, creating aerial waterfalls, and sounds out thunderous fireworks galore.

Part my story—part words from the book. It works, I think. At least it's better than what this textbook has in it!

7:24 A.M.

Captain John said he can read the weather by watching the clouds. He also told me about some of the warning signs and how to see the wind direction change in the higher altitudes.

What! I know some Latin and just figured this out. Cirrus means a wisp or curl of hair. I guess I already knew the meanings, but I would simply know the cirrus to be wisps of a cloud that are way up high and actually made of ice crystals. I wish we had ice on the boat.

Cumulus means little pile…Cumulus clouds are far from being little! A little pile of cotton candy! I need a snack—be right back.

I found peanut M&Ms! Back to cumulus—these are the white fluffy clouds that I can imagine animal shapes and creatures within their floating fluff. I see an elephant right now!

Nimbus clouds are the sign of rain. On the *Sharon*

Ann, we would watch nimbus clouds way off in the distance with super thin lines drawn straight down from the cloud to the ocean. It was super cool to see those at a distance. I haven't seen any "rain clouds" since Cape Eleuthera, but I am sure we will see more soon. They always pop up on the ocean.

Stratus is the prefix for layer in Latin. Those clouds are more like a blanket—actually, these are the clouds I imagine my Grandma Ruth up in heaven sitting on while looking down on me. She died of cancer when I was seven. It was one of the worst things in my whole life. I wonder what she would have said about us living on a sailboat, because she wasn't a sailor. She was a rancher, a cowgirl, and a philanthropist who gave to charitable organizations. She loved all four-legged creatures and told me what a philanthropist was and what an important job it is for everyone to have or do. She was super smart and graduated from Stanford where she met my grandfather, whom I never met because he died before I was born. I think they are both smiling down on us right now and keeping us safe. I've always thought that when you think of a person who has passed, they must be visiting you at that same moment. At least I hope that is true.

One can truly get lost in the sky while out on a boat! But enough of this book, it's heavy and boring, and I don't really need it for writing in my journal. I'm going to stash it back in my cabin. Be right back.

I ran into Mom in the galley, and she said if I was done with Science, I needed to read a chapter in History—so, more clouds it is!

8:00 A.M.

We changed our course settings after passing our marker point past the end of Eleuthera and halfway to Little San Salvador Island, which is our next planned stop before Cat Island. Pointing our bow farther downwind and now riding the waves, Captain John popped up from below with the spinnaker sail. I took the helm as Dad and Captain John hoisted the sail. Her sail shape was formed as the wind found her frame, among the sounds of winches, lines tightening, and the last pop of the sail before she was filled. The sail pulled us forward and over each swell. A strange calm settled on us when we left the strong winds behind us and the ocean's temper faded.

9:07 A.M.

SAILING, SOMEWHERE BETWEEN ELEUTHERA AND LITTLE SAN SALVADOR ISLAND, THE BAHAMAS

The wind is now behind us, so Captain John and Dad have rigged up this crazy "ride" for DJ and me to try. This is the "spinnaker sail ride"— totally more fun than any ride at any fair. Once the spinnaker sail was attached to the spinnaker halyard and winched halfway up the mast, then the bosun chair was attached to the holes in the bottom of the triangle-shaped spinnaker sail called clews. The bosun chair is a canvas chair used to climb the mast, but today it was attached to both bottom clews of the sail. We must have the perfect light sailing wind from behind the boat for it to work. The perfect amount to set the sail flying, but not too much to send us flying, if you know what I mean. DJ always went first, but I was totally fine with this because if anything wasn't hooked up right, he was the one to find out, not me!

When it was my turn, I climbed into the bosun chair already attached to the spinnaker sail. I climbed over the safety railing and when the wind picked up, the sail lifted me into the air. Once in a while, the wind would die down completely, and I ended up getting dunked into the water. When this happened, I would kick myself free from the bosun seat and swim back to the dive platform and start again. I was more worried about having too much wind because it seemed like I could get tossed up higher than the main mast. Well, maybe, but hopefully not. We are sailing in about a hundred feet of water, and I was more scared of getting tossed high than I was of swimming with huge fish I couldn't see. What is wrong with me?! This is so totally rad!

I guess I forgot—we did have a line attached to the bottom of the sail to keep us off to the side of the boat, so if something did go wrong, we could be dropped into the water, and the sail wouldn't end up under the boat. We had our life vests on too, and the *Western Star* was under motor, enabling Dad or Captain John to stop the boat quickly if needed. You guessed it—they had to convince me it was safe before I tried it! It was nearly impossible to go higher than twenty feet—at least, I hoped. I am not scared of most things, but this ride was terrifying, but the thrill was worth it.

I survived the spinnaker ride, and I WILL DO IT AGAIN!

The sound of the sonar rang out again, starting the grumbling of adults. From the cockpit, I could hear voices below deck. Dad and Captain John argued over nautical charts and the chart books, which are supposedly updated regularly. I've heard this saying and it fits now: "There is one thing for sure. Plans made sailing are usually tossed out into the wind."

It sounds like our plans might not only be in the wind, but we may be sunk.

CHAPTER 7

SCUBA MONSTERS

DECEMBER 8, 1979
SAILING AROUND LITTLE SAN SALVADOR ISLAND, THE BAHAMAS

December 8th is here, and I want to mark this day as a halfway point for going back to the States and finally getting to see all of my four-legged friends. I hope to see all of them, but I already know that some I will never see again. At least Mom and Dad keep DJ and me busy; the days seem to slip away from all of us. This is ISLAND time!

DECEMBER 9, 1979

I don't know when I overheard Mom and Dad talking, but I know that Captain John was hired because of his "expertise" of the islands and reefs. But then came Hurricane David, a huge category 5 hurricane that hit Puerto Rico, the Dominican Republic, Cuba, and The Bahamas, destroying everything in its path. These are all the places we planned on going, all but Cuba, anyway. I remember hearing Mom talking about it, and I knew how worried she was about Dad being in Florida during Hurricane David. This is what postponed our trip by a few weeks and caused our late departure from California. At the time, I was thankful we didn't have to leave when we had planned because it gave me more time to say my goodbyes to my furry friends. I was able to show at another horse show, and showing horses is what I like to do.

I miss the smell of my horses' and my ponies' noses, the smell of the barn when I first walk inside, and the smell of alfalfa at feeding time. I miss their soft gentle nickers, the feeling of their muzzle in my hands. High Hopes, one of my show horses, smells me from my right toes up to my nose and back down the other side, sniffing out hidden carrots. I miss their gentle head nudges against my body, asking for the carrot pieces they smell in my pockets. The only one I have to watch out for is my sweet, adorable Vicky. She can act like the sweetest pony in the whole world and in an instant take a chunk of skin in her teeth and yank it and me across the stall. Witchy Vicky is her nickname from Mom. Vicky actually bit my butt so hard once that I couldn't sit for days and had to sleep on my stomach with an icepack on it. Even at her worst, I love her the most. I miss her probably the most but never tell the others, Sweet Pea, Dolly, High Hopes, Coconut, or Split Second. They would be jealous! When I grow up, I want to be a horse trainer. I can't see me doing anything else.

Dad's so mad at Captain John over the charts, I hear them almost yelling. Dad decided we should anchor out near Little San Salvador Island for the night, but at day-break we were heading to Cat Island. We seem to have circled around the island and finally as we sailed slowly toward Little San Salvador, the wind kept my hair up above my shoulders, swirling uncontrollably. Speaking of hurricanes, my hair was as if it were in a hurricane above and around my head. I am tempted to find a knife and cut it off, but a rubber band will do because I don't want to look like a boy.

Dad still didn't trust the charts, and the closer we approached Little San Salvador, it seemed like the alarms would sound louder and the depth finder would read 2 fathoms, 10 fathoms, .5 fathoms. They seemed to be bouncing from eighteen feet to six feet of water in a matter of seconds. It seems Hurricane David decided to make changes above ground and under. The night was spent being rocked to sleep with the occasional off roll, just enough to toss someone out of a bunk with a bang. With any luck, it will be DJ and not me getting tossed to the cabin floor.

Captain John was on watch the first few hours, and then Dad relieved him. The scary thing that happens at night is that the shore looks closer than it really is, making it seem as if the boat is drifting toward shore. It's really freaky, and I didn't want to go to sleep. I sat and watched the island for hours before falling to sleep.

7:00 A.M.

LEAVING LITTLE SAN SALVADOR ISLAND, THE BAHAMAS

The sound of heavy footsteps above my bunk woke me from a deep sleep. Looking out the porthole to the horizon, I see miles and miles of nothing but ocean. It was really weird that there were no waves and the ocean was totally flat. Suddenly the humming of the anchor winch whined, the anchor line being coiled slapped the inside of the anchor, thunk, thunk, thunk repeating until the sound of the anchor chain clanked and rattled against the anchor guides as it crawled and banged against the chain roller and through the chain pawl. I leapt off the bunk and changed my clothes, brushed my teeth with my cup of water, tried my best to brush my wild blonde mane, and then French-braided it as quickly as I could. As I headed out toward the hatch, I noticed the nautical charts spread out over the dinner table. It was dark, and I could hardly make out what charts were open, but assumed they were the same as yesterday. It was so early. I heard more footsteps on deck and the familiar sound of winches reeled to raise the main and the jib. The boat hardly rocked, I noticed, as I climbed the steps to the cockpit.

I watched the sunrise. I might have been half sleeping, but the orange colors seemed to have been smeared from the water into the sky and the bright orange burning ball rose from the water right beside the island, turning the island and everything on it black, like a shadow. It was totally rad! After, I snuck down to see the charts below.

I measured out Cat Island's length on the chart, finding it's about fifty nautical miles long—maybe, if my calculations are correct. Again, I can be so off. I think I am getting better at reading charts or at least at measuring distances and islands. But once again, I am positive that if I had to calculate our headings we would end up on the other side of the world. The place directly on the other side of the world from us would probably be Western Australia. Yep, that's where I would navigate us to if I were in charge of the navigation. I wonder if I will ever figure out navigating. That's why I wouldn't trust myself with the navigation.

Dad sat down with such a thud, the cushion next to me sank. He stared at the charts and twisted and rolled his beard between his thumb and pointing finger. This is what he does when he's nervous. I didn't ask why we weren't going to stay at Little San Salvador Island. I just sat.

7:14 A.M.
SAILING. LITTLE SAN SALVADOR TO CAT ISLAND, THE BAHAMAS

The bow pitched and dipped, rose and fell as the space between my toes and the top of the water got closer, and then up we went again. My short legs dangled off the edge of the pulpit as I leaned forward, pushing my body forward against the pulpit rails. I reached my arms toward the water, amazed at its bright blue colors. On the port side, the water is a bright azure blue. The water is clear and clean, and the shapes of the coral below us are just a blur as we sail over them. But off our starboard side, the water is a deep royal blue. It's like a line formed deep below us, drawn by the currents and probably Hurricane David, plus all the hurricanes before him. Cat Island is off in the distance. We are heading toward her but keeping her on our port side, heading south. I think I will read. It's a perfect day!

CAT ISLAND, THE BAHAMAS
24.229268, -75.420172

How do you anchor in a bed of sand? The loose sand wouldn't hold a huge boat in place if the wind picked up. We typically can leave all the anchor chain on the sandy ocean floor and the weight helps hold the boat in place when anchored out. It's funny, the wind can change in the middle of the night, pushing the boat 90 degrees. You went to bed with the island on the port side, and in the morning, it's on the starboard side. Some mornings I wake up feeling lost for the first moments until I get my bearings. You might feel the same way if someone came into your room and moved your bed to the other side of your room while you were asleep.

After our anchor was secured, I sat down on deck looking toward the beach. Its pink sand seemed to reach both ends of the world, not a human, boat, house, or hut in sight. I heard two splashes off the dive platform and saw Dad and DJ headed toward the anchor with their dive gear on. The water is so clear I could see every detail of them, their tanks, and each air bubble floating up to the surface. The sound of Mom's laugh caught my ear from only a few steps away. She was laughing so hard, she had tears in her eyes and couldn't speak, but she pointed. Two eyes—very, very wide black eyes—were staring at me, and then with a sudden dash, she was gone. I tiptoed closer to where she had darted off. Peeking over the Jet Ski, I noticed Baby-Bear's wide black eyes as they met mine. She dashed off to the other side of the Jet Ski. I continued this peekaboo game with BabyBear for several minutes until she was done and sat on one of the cushions next to Mom in the cockpit and groomed herself in the sun. After her short grooming session, BabyBear was off roaming the upper deck, inspecting every inch. She was daring today and even peeked over the side of the boat, looking down into the water at her new friends, schools of fish. BabyBear followed a sound until she noticed the bubbles popping at the water's surface. This intrigued her, until the two monsters broke surface and BabyBear went skidding around the deck, making her way at mach speed down the hatch. I am sure she hid deep inside the aft cabin. We didn't see her again for hours. Poor BabyBear, traumatized by the scuba monsters. Well, who wouldn't be scared of DJ, in or out of scuba gear?

DJ gets to scuba dive, and I get handed a chore—not fair! Swab the deck, Matey! Captain John handed me a mop and bucket with soap and water, so I started mopping and singing. "Hi Ho, Hi Ho, off to work I go, I'll swab the deck, try not to break my neck, Hi Ho, Hi Ho."

The thick layers of salt were washing away with each swipe. By the time I was done, Captain John was rinsing her off, and she was gleaming. Job completed and all sudsy myself, I jumped overboard. It was totally awesome. My body, floating free. I rolled over to my back and floated with the hundreds of rainbow bubbles I'd created while mopping. So, this is heaven, or at least how I pictured what heaven would be like.

CHAPTER 8

SCUBA DIVING AND THE GREAT RACE

DECEMBER 25, 1979

CAT ISLAND, THE BAHAMAS

24.229268, -75.420172

Merry Christmas! What a beautiful day to celebrate such a special day.

Living on the *Western Star* has taught me to appreciate everything. Everything people living on land don't appreciate, or at least I didn't! What I appreciate and miss the most about living in a house, besides my pets, is fresh water! Wait, *unlimited* fresh water. We were lucky to have a water maker on board and able to share water with other people. A few days ago, people anchored their sailboat near us and swam over to ask Dad where they could get some water. Yes, this really happened. Dad told them to bring over their container and he would fill it up. Until that moment, I didn't realize how important the water maker really was. I know I took it for granted even though we didn't have one on the *Sharon Ann*. I had forgotten how difficult it was without drinking water. As I watched, the two of them swam toward us with their jugs and then Dad filled their containers and took them back to their dinghy-less boat. I became more thankful at that moment for our dinghy…our dry and quick ride to shore, or in this case, a dry ride to the boat next door.

Other things I miss about living in a house are a telephone, going out to dinner or fast food restaurants, being dry, washing clothes whenever you need to, and ice—oh, yes, I miss ICE! And let me not forget about being able to go to a store to buy anything and being able to go at any time!

It's Christmas—what was I thinking? I should have bought gifts, not made little trinkets, speaking of not being able to go shop. I made DJ a little line-knot keychain, but I think it will only remind him that he's not home and able to drive a car. He will bruise my arm terribly for this. Mom will never wear this necklace I made of tiny shells and fishing line. Why wasn't I more thoughtful? And Dad…I only drew him a pencil drawing of coconut palms on a beach. It's the only thing I can draw half decently. Captain John…well, what do you make for a guy who taught you to navigate with the stars and read your surroundings to predict the weather? I wrote him this:

STAR LIGHT, STAR BRIGHT,

NORTH STAR, I SEE YOUR GUIDING LIGHT.

WILL YOU PLEASE HELP GUIDE OUR WAY,

SO WE WILL NOT GO ASTRAY?

A DARK MYSTERIOUS NIMBUS CLOUD,

YOU TELL US A STORY LOUD AND PROUD.

IF THE WIND STARTS SQUALLING,

SOON RAIN MAY BE FALLING.

TRUE SAILORS NEVER COMPLAIN.

FORGIVE ME IF THIS IS LAME.

ONLY CIRRUS CLOUDS IN THE MIX.

RELAX AND HAVE SOME KICKS.

IT'S CHRISTMAS DAY.

ENJOY THIS BEAUTIFUL BAY!

Lame is an understatement! How do I thank someone for sharing their skills with me? Besides a simple thank you, I haven't a clue. The patience it takes to teach someone like me, this alone is a talent.

On this boat, I have learned to navigate with charts and by using the stars and the horizon. I wish we had a sunstone, the navigational crystal the Vikings used. Dad told me they were the sextants in the Viking period. I have also learned to see the position of the sun and use it as my watch to tell time. The weather can be predicted in the clouds, the wind, and currents. Every day has been a new lesson and a gift, but I have no way of giving anything in return. What should I do? I guess I should have thought this out before today.

Skipping Christmas, at least the gift part, should have been an option! After breakfast, Dad said that our gifts are waiting for us in Puerto Rico. That's a few months away! Did I say I am learning patience? That doesn't mean I have any yet.

DECEMBER 26, 1979

If there were such a place on Earth close to heaven, seriously, I think we found it! It didn't seem to matter at all that I already feel salty and grimy. I woke up this morning and saw the prettiest beach I've ever seen. I tried to move after waking up on deck, every part of me hurting from the hard surface, like I'd slept on a boulder or a concrete driveway. I know, not much of a bed, but the cool air, the sounds of birds, and an occasional splash from a large fish feeding close to the water's surface makes it seem all are saying, "Good morning." Plus, I am not in the cabin with DJ!

The sun is low, and its soft rays began warming me from the cool morning air. I looked down at the sea floor, the details amazingly clear. I smelled coffee. Captain John was awake and sitting in the cockpit. I felt like plopping into the water but have learned that the water temperature drops overnight and it would be cold! It would definitely awaken every inch of my body, probably with a blow. I heard a sound coming from behind the boat and saw water movement, like little ripples. I stood to see what it was, then wobbled toward the stern of the boat. A flipper attached to a leg…it was my dad, up early scrubbing the hull. He always swims in the morning before we all wake up. I wish I could be dedicated to do something like that every day. Well, I guess I do, but it involves horses, and seahorses don't count. Dad qualified for the Olympics in the butterfly a long, long, time ago. He didn't compete. I was told it was because at that time Olympians had to pay their own way. Maybe if he'd gone, I wouldn't be here, so all things happen for a reason.

I decided to go for a morning swim. Well, more like a morning float.

DECEMBER 28, 1979

Between my toes, the tiny granular bits of pinkish sand gather. I swipe it with my hands but realize it covers most of my drying body. It's pink! It reminds me of a fifth-place ribbon. I've never felt sand as soft or seen sand this pink. It's hard to believe this is sand! I started to pile it on top of my legs, creating pant legs, but it's not like California sand that packs up nicely to make shapes and castles. So I dug my feet and hands into it, digging until I felt the cool sand below.

Mom spread her towel next to mine after her long walk down the never-ending beach. We saw no humans on this beach—no one! I looked out onto the water toward the *Western Star*. She seemed to be floating in air, the water was so clear and still. It is super cool.

The sound of birds from the trees behind us is pretty loud. Probably seagulls hoping for a handout. The coconut palms in the breeze are the only sounds heard besides the squawk from Mr. and Mrs. Seagull. It is strange to sit on a beach and not hear the water lapping against the shore. That's what Mom calls it when the water's waves break onto the beach. Besides the few birds and the breeze in the trees, it is quiet until I hear Dad's and Captain John's voices coming from the *Western Star*. Their voices seem closer than they are. I'm going to see what's going on; be right back.

1:00 P.M.

I watched as Captain John and Dad jumped down into the dinghy, which sank into the water with an oomph sound. The still water rippled like it was racing away from the dinghy and then splashed up against the *Western Star's* hull. Captain John untied the line as Dad started the motor. Mom and I watched them drive down the shore, passing us without a wave. They beached the dinghy, running it up onto the beach while simultaneously tilting the engine up out of the water so it didn't hit the sand and break the shaft off. Captain John had a bag in his hand, but I could hardly make out what it was. He walked up toward the sandy dirt road, at least it seemed to be a road or path, and he disappeared.

Wait! Gone, like the tutor? I hope not! Captain John and I spend lots of time studying the stars. He knows how to navigate using the stars, almost more than using charts. He sneaks sailing terms and uses sailing tricks only a seasoned sailor would know. I have learned so much about sailing from him. He reads the weather by the looks of clouds and the feel and direction of the wind, and he can feel the moisture in the air and notice current changes. We have watched storms moving across the open water, the shapes of the storm and its direction, together. He says it can be a lifesaving element if you know how to read the wind, water, clouds, and currents. We sit on deck talking about these things for hours. It is totally cool.

One thing I have always noticed...he is protective over his drinking cup! The later it gets in the day, the more often he goes down to his cabin to fill his cup again. Typically, he laughs at DJ and me, and I've seen him almost in tears, even when he has his aviator sunglasses on. What is in the cup? I don't care. It's his and his business alone, but he doesn't share.

After Mom and I snorkeled off the beach for a little while, we went back to the beach and waited for a ride back to the boat. I knew I would find out where Captain John went because Mom is more curious than I am, and she will have Dad tell her everything.

LATE AFTERNOON, BACK ABOARD THE WESTERN STAR

Captain John arrived back at the beach with his bag. He whistled for a ride, and DJ being on deck, he jumped down to the dinghy, untied, and off he went. Seeing Captain John was like seeing an uncle. I was glad he was back. He'd gone into town for some supplies, cigarettes, and whisky was what he told me. This was not the answer I thought I would hear but the answer to several questions I once had!

1980!!!!

HAPPY NEW YEAR! A NEW YEAR AND BIRTHDAY CELEBRATIONS

Dad blew out his candles. I think he has his wish, all of us being on the *Western Star*.

I blew out my candles and wished to be with Honey-Bear and Vicky. Guess what? It didn't happen. During my long walk on the beach today I daydreamed Vicky was here so we could canter down the beach and splash in the water. I bet she would have loved this calm water and would have gone for a swim. At the Del Mar beach, we would watch the racehorses run along the shoreline and then go for a swim. Little Vicky wanted nothing to do with the surf! It's days like today, I wish I were home.

JANUARY 2, 1980
CAT ISLAND, SCUBA DIVING LESSON, THE BAHAMAS

Off to the beach, where I learned more basics of scuba diving! My father always said he would like to wait until I could at least walk with the tank on my back, but I am the size of a peanut. The thirty-five-pound tank continued to get the best of me. Top- and back-heavy, I found myself being forced downward into the sand. My feet sank deeper as the weight drove my feet down into the sand like fence posts being set into place back on the ranch. My BC (buoyancy compensator) is like a life vest, but the air can be emptied for the dive or refilled to float on the surface. It's also connected to the air tank on my back. It felt like an adult shell on a baby turtle's back. Dad had to help steady me all the way to the water, or without his help, I would have toppled over. Dad grabbed the top of the tank and set the tank with me attached upright onto the beach. I felt like a rag doll. He kept me on my feet as I wobbled my way into the water. I was thankful the weight of the water makes the sand almost as hard as concrete, as this made walking easier. DJ found the whole ordeal humorous and was practically crying at the sight of me. I was so mad that I would have hit him if I knew I wouldn't fall on my butt again. On the other hand, maybe I should have tried.

The deeper the water got, the easier walking became, and the tank was much easier to deal with in the water. I filled my BC "vest" up and floated in about three feet of water with my feet anchoring me in place and my hands wrapped around my BC vest, keeping it from swallowing my head.

Dad ran through the lessons and then another quick

review of the rules. We checked the air pressure gauge, checked both regulators again, and added a couple hand signals to review before we moved on to the next stage. As I secured my mask and slid the snorkel off to the side, making sure it didn't flop around, I reached for the regulator and stuck the mouthpiece in my mouth. I started breathing through the regulator above water and quickly realized what I was doing. I stuck my head under and followed Dad down below the surface. The first five feet, I struggled a bit, just like I did free diving. But after five feet, the pressure of the water helped keep me steady, and I didn't have to try as hard to swim deeper. I could picture it—the life of a mermaid!

I was comfortable breathing underwater. It seemed natural. Dad stopped me and added a few lessons in the shallow water. Dad, as a certified PADI dive master and instructor, made sure I was safe and checked to see if I remembered all the prior lessons taught. We ventured off to some close reefs. Dad had said that Cat Island is a great place to learn to dive and warned me of tests he would do with me and not to worry, he was right by my side. These tests would let him know if I can stay calm in emergencies. I guess they would show him if I would ask for help or panic.

Besides the huge tank that felt much heavier than thirty-five pounds above water, diving was easy, and when I was breathing from my regulator, it didn't freak me out knowing I was ten to twenty feet under and breathing in tank air. I am still confused how they compress air to get it into a tank, but it's super awesome to breathe under water!

We swam deeper than I thought we would on my first day. I even had to clear my ears. This is when you go under the water and your ears feel pressure pushing in on your eardrums. Goggles have a nose-shaped rubber piece over your nose so you can hold your nose with your fingers. If you blow gently out of your nose while holding your nose shut, you can unclog your ears. Cool, right?

As we traveled a little deeper, the water become a little darker blue and little colder. I looked at my depth gauge, and it showed we were only eighteen feet below the surface. But we swam down deeper. Once I cleared my ears, and my mask filled with water. I found it amusing to fix my mask underwater. Dad said some people apparently panic, but I have never had the stinging sensation from saltwater in my eyes, so maybe the fear of not having a mask on didn't faze me. In my opinion, saltwater feels much better than a pool's chlorine water. Blowing air bubbles out my nose filled my mask back up with air. This was so rad. Some people see challenges…I see fun and entertainment. It's always the little things.

I felt so confident for the first thirty minutes, I was ready to explore the coral reef and go wreck diving. My eyes scanned the sandy ocean floor below us, and I found some larger fish to follow and soon found some rock, coral, and really bright colored fish. Unlike snorkeling near the surface, what I saw were larger fish than the little one- to two-inch clown fish. We also saw several colors of butterfly fish. We spotted a grouper I nicknamed Dinner. We saw several angelfish that looked a foot long. Hidden near the sandy bottom were a couple stingrays cruising around. I could have stayed there all day!

The sound of my breathing through the regulator became less intense. My mind was on the fish, the coral, and the living creatures all around us, not the sounds coming from the regulator in my mouth or the bubbles rising all around my face. The angelfish seemed to stare back at me, almost as intensely as I stared at them. Several schools of fish swam with me and then would pass me. I studied their bright colors as they danced in unison.

Then something happened. A flash of unknown. Fear I have never felt before. It was as if I were sucking a straw that someone had pinched closed. My regulator lost air. I panicked. I had no air. Quicker than my mind could go, I guess I automatically grabbed my octopus—the spare regulator—my thought was *this will work*. But I sucked and nothing. I looked for Dad. He must have seen my panicked look. I signed "No Air" toward him, and it felt like everything was going in slow motion. My mouth was now filled with water, so I spit it out. All I could think of was, *I need air!* First, I looked toward Dad, and it seemed like he was a mile away. I looked up to see how deep we were and thought surfacing might be my best bet. I looked up once more and suddenly a regulator appeared and was jammed into my hand and mouth. I gasped and held my nose. I have no idea why I held my nose, but I am glad I did! I was okay, but my eyes filled with tears. Dad and I moved slowly upward to the surface as I tried to control my breathing. I could feel my heart thumping so hard and so fast. I was scared and super bummed I wasn't really a mermaid after all.

My tank had malfunctioned, and it wasn't a test! Dad was able to swap it with DJ's, and we went back down as DJ snorkeled above us. I kept one eye on him and followed Dad down to about twenty-five feet. We stopped, and he signed asking if all was okay? I was good, but I felt scared. We slowly made our way back and up to the beach.

Dad made me "climb back on the horse that bucked me off," and if he hadn't, I might never have gone scuba diving again!

JANUARY 8, 1980
ANOTHER DAY AT CAT ISLAND, THE BAHAMAS

Today's chore was cleaning the head—being so small, it should be one of the easiest of chores, right? Needless to say, the part of sharing the head with two men rates this chore the worst ever. I would much rather wipe all the teak down belowdecks, sweep the floors, scrub or mop the whole boat deck, reroll all the lines, or sand and varnish the teak on deck, all in one day. Matter of fact, I would rather scrub the hull with a scrub brush while trying to balance in the dinghy than clean the head. I hate chores! I want to go home!

JANUARY 10, 1980

There is no better way to spend a day than racing DJ on the Jet Skis—that's since we are making it a bet! There is little to no way I will win, but with some luck I can. There's crystal clear, glassy calm water as always here on Cat Island. We are two very competitive siblings. We are racing for "swapping a chore day." I don't know what chore DJ hates the most. He doesn't seem to like any of them.

The odds are in his favor because he is skilled, brave, and a daredevil, and I only learned how to ride these a few months ago. Well, I guess we both did, but he raced motocross and BMX bikes before that. I am so light I could find myself skipping across the water instead of racing through it. The last time I rode, I took a hard fall that was worse than a horse bucking me off. I skidded and skipped across the water like a skipping rock, and when I landed, it was on the side of my head, onto my ear. My ear hurt for days after that crash. I was surprised it wasn't bleeding, or worse.

I think I slept for a couple days straight after that fall. But I can't think of that! I have to think of it as NOT cleaning the head for a day.

The race is on. Challenge accepted! I am in it to win it!

2:00 P.M.

DJ punched me in the arm so hard I couldn't pick up a pen. I had to eat left handed, although that has never been a problem, but writing with my left hand is terribly difficult. Oh, the race! That's why he hit me.

I was practically left in the dust, or should I say ocean spray, at the start. I followed in his wake, and it seemed to slow me down even more, but after we both made the turn and I got out of his backwash, I noticed I was catching up to him. He kept turning around and saying things like, "Later, Scatter" and "Eat my dust." We both had the throttles fully open, the gas full flowing, the pedal to the metal—we were at full speed! DJ was standing, and I was sitting low on my knees, keeping a low profile. Yeah, that's what Dad called it. Even the turn was smooth and sharp. He turned on a dime, jumping his wake. I heard the hum of his engine as he floated in the air. I kept my Jet Ski low and in the water. Soon I found myself nose to nose with DJ, and he swerved toward me a few times to try to scare me, but all it did was slow himself down. My hands are still aching from squeezing the throttle and gripping the handlebars so hard.

Needless to say, I won the race, and DJ punched me in the arm when we reached the boat. Dad ignored the punch and said I won the race because I am so light and kept my body profile down, leaving no drag. Okay, whatever...I won! DJ accused me of cheating, and that was that. I have to say, the race and the win were so much fun!!! We left the Jet Skis in the water so we can ride around tomorrow. Even though he's pissed now, we found some really cool inlets we want to explore. That is, if he will still speak to me tomorrow.

CHAPTER 9

TREASURE HUNT

JANUARY 12, 1980

CAT ISLAND, THE BAHAMAS

We grilled tonight, and after dinner, I grabbed my blanket and pillow and found my favorite spot on deck. Looking into the sky, the moon seems to have swallowed the stars and has ventured closer for a better look at Earth.

Splash! A large fish jumped from the water near the side of the *Western Star*. The shoreline seems closer to us than usual, the pinkish sand close enough to hop on. I see a long pole-shaped shadow resting on the sand, running toward the shoreline. It's the mast of the *Western Star*. I stood to see more, and more of the details of the mast stood out. I can even see some of the lines attached. Weird! The Jet Skis are floating behind the boat but now look as if they are floating in air, space-like, casting perfect shadows onto the ocean floor. So slick!

A fish swam near the boat without a water ripple, or wave or blur. BabyBear looked over the cockpit edge trying to sneak up on me, only to play her favorite game of hide-and-seek. Her eyes black as coal, her little tail flops against the deck, and her butt does a little wiggle as she crouches down, readying for the kill…her prey is me! She lunges toward me and lands on all four feet, hunched up like a Halloween cat. Bounce, bounce, bounce, and she leaps back toward the cockpit and tears off in a hurry. Shhh! She is hiding again.

I tiptoed down the deck to find her, and another fish jumped. The splashes got BabyBear's full attention. She was on the hunt, but not for me, for fresh fish! In the moonlight, the fish didn't even look like they were in water—air maybe, but not swimming in water. There are no words to describe what I saw! BabyBear's eyes were pinned on these fish critters. Her little butt wiggled, and her tail slapped the deck. She held her low profile stance and then with one quick lunge… I yelled as she plunged off the side of the *Western Star* and into the water. The ocean rippled, with BabyBear splashing.

Mom and I yelled but stood like we were in cement. Thank goodness for Dad's lifeguarding skills, because before I could blink, Dad had BabyBear back on deck and was wrapping her up in a towel. Then he handed the water-soaked towel holding a very mad little kitty to Mom. After Mom dried her off and let her go, BabyBear licked and licked that salty water off her fur. She made the funniest faces, like she was licking a lemon slice. Poor BabyBear, and she had been having so much fun playing hide-and-seek.

JANUARY 16, 1980
DAYS TURNED TO WEEKS, CAT ISLAND, THE BAHAMAS

Dad told us stories of buried treasure on this island. "A pirate named Arthur Catt, a good friend of the famous Blackbeard pirate, in the late 1600s and early 1700s often came to these waters. He made this island his home away from home. Pirate Catt hid treasures in the hills and in caves here on San Salvador, not Little San Salvador but San Salvador. The treasure was never found. Much later, in the mid 1920s, San Salvador Island was renamed to Cat Island after Pirate Catt himself. Maybe the locals thought if they renamed the island, the treasure would reveal itself. Oh, why only one T for the spelling of Cat Island is unknown"—but really Dad didn't even know.

Dad continued, "Maybe it has something to do with the fact that black magic was used by the locals on this island. Obeah spells were done for both healing and other positive outcomes. However, enemies be warned, Obeah curses were cast as well. Hidden behind this beautiful beach are water inlets. Waterways to the unknown, the unexplored, or, as I see it, waterways to Pirate Catt's hidden treasure."

Dad went on for about an hour telling us about pirates and treasure. I was a bit freaked out over the black-magic stuff, but then Dad said we may even find a pirate ship while diving around these islands. How cool would that be? Way, way cool!

DJ and I looked at each other and knew it was time to go check out the hidden waterways.

JANUARY 17, 1980

DJ and I decided last night after doing our chores that

today would be the for venturing off into hidden canals on our Jet Skis. We have treasure to find.

In the shallow water in some of the inlets, it was too difficult to stand while going so slow. So I had to drop to my knees on the deck. Being lower to the water made it difficult to see what lurked below, but falling off wasn't an option! I guess we should have been looking below us for treasure, but everything looked strange and kind of freaky. The mangrove roots looked like dried octopus legs, and I got the creeps just riding near them. We had only a foot of clearance on both sides of our Jet Skis in some places. These canals were much smaller than the ones we'd explored on Paradise Island.

DJ took the lead as always, but this time I didn't care because if there was going to be any danger, he would be the first to ride into it. He was fearless cruising through shallow and sometimes very dark, even black waters. I, on the other hand, had shivers run through my bones, sending millions of tiny goosebumps up and down my arms and leaving the hair on my arms stretched out. The hairs stood out so straight they didn't look like they wanted to stay attached to my arm. The water was still, and everything was quiet except for the deep-toned gurgling sounds of our Jet Ski motors. We reached a passageway that split, and I wondered how DJ picked which way to go. My mind concentrated on staying on the Jet Ski and not getting stuck in one of the mangrove plants. The mangrove's large octopus-like roots routed themselves deep down into the water and sternly into the canal's floor; not even a hurricane can uproot one of these bad boys. A large osprey launched up into the air from seemingly nowhere, shouting and squawking at us. We probably interrupted his mangrove tree crab lunch. I am sure we scared him. Well, I have news, he scared me more!

Our eyes should have been looking for treasure, but I couldn't stop staring at the water below us. When the water cleared, there were tons of super small fish of all shapes and sizes. Thank goodness I had forgotten about the baby sharks and that 90 percent of all sea critters' babies hide in the mangroves until they are large enough to be safe out at sea. We had circled around, but still saw nothing. After leaving one canal, DJ and I raced down the shoreline, and I followed him right back into another canal. As my mother would say, "If he was leading you off a cliff, would you follow?" Today, apparently, I would, because there is a treasure to be found.

After an hour, maybe, we made our way out of the inlets and mangrove canals. It was so good to be out of there, but we didn't find any treasure. At least we looked.

When we arrived back at the *Western Star*, Dad was so mad. What DJ and I didn't think about was if something had happened to us, Dad had no way of getting to us. He told us he didn't know if there were crocodiles in the lakes back behind the inlets. Freaked me out! What were those dark areas underneath our Jet Skis that caused my arm hairs to stand up? Say what?! Every inch of my body was quivering, but I quickly shook it off. Dude!

JANUARY 20, 1980

We leave Cat Island tomorrow and are heading to Conception Island. Days have run into weeks, weeks into months. I believe we have fallen into island time! No due dates or deadlines, simply a gas gauge and a craving for fresh vegetables and fruit, and definitely the need for chocolate! It is time to head to an island with a marina. Plus, I am sure Granny has been worried about us for the past few weeks, so Dad will need to find a phone to tell her about our adventures while parked at one of the many ocean parking lots. But the need for chocolate is number one on my list!

Dad was able to make a ship-to-shore call, but the radio was heavy with static, and it took thirty minutes to place the call. Someone on shore got the information from Dad and then tried to make the call and kept trying until someone answered. Then she was hard to understand, so Granny had a hard time knowing what was going on. We could hear Granny, but she couldn't hear us and then when she finally could hear, between the static and talking at the same time, it was nearly impossible to understand. Not too many people know you can't talk over radios at the same time or if we have the button pushed down to talk, we can't hear. Plus, Granny couldn't understand why Dad kept saying, "over" at the end of every statement. "Over" was used to let the other person know that you were done talking and the other person was free to speak. Then the word "copy" is used when you understand what they are saying. I thought everyone knew this, but it's only a boat and truck driver thing, I guess. Apparently, the call was very expensive, so I think they will stick to calling her from landlines. But let's remember, we tie up at night to floating docks in the middle of the ocean, so we can sleep. That still cracks me up! Poor Granny, if she only knew.

7:05 A.M.

COOL MORNING AIR,

WARMED BY THE SUN.

GENTLY BRUSHED IS THE SKY,

PINKS AND ORANGES ARE TO THE EAST.

SOFTLY THE SUN WHISPERS, "GOOD MORNING,"

WHILE THE OCEAN ROCKS YOU BACK TO SLEEP.

Funny right? Can you tell I had to work on literature books basically all day? Yes, it needs LOTS more work, but I thought I would share.

9:40 A.M.

I folded my blanket and stuck my pillow on top of the pile. I waited in the swing chair still hanging off the boom, stretched out over the port side of the boat! What a great place to go when I feel the need to get away from everyone on this boat. Or, like this morning, a comfortable place to chill. I pulled the little line attached to the PVC plastic piped arm on the swing chair and brought the meshed covered seat up close to the wire railing near me. I couldn't reach the seat well enough to get in using one hand, so I needed to figure out how was I going to leap into the chair with a pen and notebook. Without the pen and notebook it would still be hard, so I decided to lower the line from the boom that held the swing chair up. This would make the chair lower to the water but easier for me to reach the PVC-piped frame to get in. I cleated the line off, securing the swing chair so that it wouldn't drop into the water. The chair now reached closer to the deck, so that was a success.

I thought I could hold the PVC pipe closest to the mesh seat with one hand and the railing for balance with the other hand, then let go of the railing and hop into the seat as it swung down. I had to put the journal down! I stepped over the railing, holding on to the flimsy wire railing with one hand and the other hand on the swing chair. I decided to swing out facing the seat with my knees on the plastic PVC pipe that frames the seat, and once I let go of the wire railing on the boat, I could grab the PVC frame on both the sides. When the chair stopped swinging, I could turn around to sit. My feet were shaking as I balanced on the edge of the slippery deck, and the only thing left to do was go for it. I stepped off the edge of the *Western Star* and was riding the chair down over the water as planned. I almost yelled as I dropped with the swing, but before I could get a yelp out, the small line grabbed hold. The seat stopped mid-swing, and I didn't. Off I flew. I catapulted out and into the water with my PJs on! Oh, was it cold! I looked back at the boat, and everyone was on deck laughing at me. I dove under the water, though it never felt so cold! I'd forgotten to untie the little line! Dang it!

A quick change into a swimsuit, and I was then helped into the swing chair with my journal. Everyone thought it would be "hilarious" if I stayed out over the water in the chair as we made our way from the shallow bay of Cat Island to deeper seas before setting our sails, so here I sit, swinging!

With every rolling wave, my bottom dunks into the water. Have I ever told you that I am afraid of sharks and things I can't see underneath me? Well, I am! Oh, but this is hilarious! I am not amused. Well, at least I am alone and get the day off from morning chores. Now, to keep the journal dry!

CHAPTER 10

DEEP DIVE

JANUARY 21, 1980

SAILING FROM CAT ISLAND TO CONCEPTION ISLAND, THE BAHAMAS

I sat staring at the charts of Conception Island and measured out the longest side of the island. If I am correct, it's only three and a half miles long and the widest width is slightly shorter. It's almost round, unlike all the other long, skinny Bahama islands. Captain John said no one has lived on the island since the early 1900s, and it has recently been adopted as a national park. A safe place for green turtles and exotic island birds to nest. That's super cool! I can't wait to look for turtles.

Today we caught a nice mahi-mahi, or as some other people call them, dorado or dolphins. Not to worry, it's not the dolphin or porpoise we all love. These are fish that are typically caught about three to five feet long and are, well, they are hard to explain. Their backs are dark blue, their bodies are mostly green with spackles of blue and gold, and the lower section of their long body is a yellow-gold. They have one long fin running along their back, which is also dark blue, and two little fins sticking out their sides that seem way too little for their bodies. They also have a long fin hanging down from underneath, but it's closer to their head. They sparkle and change colors, but I'm not sure if they change colors to blend into their environment or what causes the change. They are amazing creatures. They are fun to reel in on a fishing line because they jump out of the water and fight the line, trying to get the hook out of their mouth. Unlike a grouper, they take off deeper and try to plant themselves under a rock or coral. Tuna takes off and they are strong and can break a line, but at least they don't dive under rocks. Swordfish are the most fun to catch, but we release most of them because they don't taste as good as mahi-mahi or tuna or grouper.

3:00 P.M.

CONCEPTION ISLAND, THE BAHAMAS

I am excited to eat our fresh mahi-mahi for dinner tonight! As we made our way into the bay, Dad drove the *Western Star* like he was driving a car on a winding road. He had to turn around coral that looked like lumps sitting there, forming new islands. Okay, not that big, but it was a little weird. We set the anchor with coral on our port side and sand off our starboard side, but in the morning, that could be the other way if the boat spins. Dad jumped into the dinghy with our extra anchor and line and set it and then brought the line back—maybe because on Cat Island we spun 360 degrees around our anchor line, and if we did that here, we would end up on the coral reef or the beach. I guess two anchors would give us a little more protection from hitting the coral reef and sinking our home.

After dinner, I hung the bag of dishes from the swim platform and watched the fish gather around for their dinner. After, I sat in the cockpit with Captain John as he stared at the beach on Conception Island. He told me that a couple years ago, he was here in the spring and sat on the deck of his boat watching as huge green sea turtles slowly pulled themselves up onto the beach. Then they dug holes in the sand, laid their eggs, and buried them. As soon as their job was done, they disappeared in the water, passing below the boat he was sitting on. He said when the weather was calm like today, he could hear birds nesting and carrying on, feeding their new babies. Birds like ospreys, snooty terns, doves, pigeons, finches, parakeets, and even parrots. How cool would it be to see wild parrots! He said he took a dinghy up the creek at high tide, through the mangroves, and told me stories about the creek. It was filled with small baby fish that live in mangroves, but the funniest story was when his boat brushed up against some mangrove plants and the mangrove tree crabs were so scared that they dropped from the plants. But instead of falling into the water, they fell into the boat, and he and his friend danced around the dinghy trying to brush the crabs back into the water and not get pinched.

There are so many different plants like sea grape, pigeon plum, gumbo-limbo, and coco plum growing up the island's hill, which was only about eighty feet above sea level. In the spring, Captain John said the hillside blooms make this the perfect place for birds to nest. He saw his first wild snake, a boa. DJ had a boa. I didn't mind holding it, but he would let it loose in my room, and it would scare me to death. I was always looking out for rattlesnakes on the ranch but not expecting a snake in my dresser drawer. DJ was so mean! Captain John said the snake was slithering around a plant just off the side of his dinghy, wrapped around branches. He couldn't tell how long the snake was, but then Captain John raised his hands, touched his pointing fingers together and his thumbs to make a circle and said it had to be at least this thick. No way—that's a huge snake. DJ's was only a couple inches round.

If only it was May or June, not January, because I would love to see the turtles nest, hear the birds talking, and maybe see a parrot. I wouldn't mind not seeing snakes.

Captain John's sea turtle story reminded me of when I was really young, like seven. We were on a trip with my grandmother Ruth. I think we were in Costa Rica, but I don't remember exactly. Anyway, I ordered the soup and thought it was so good, but DJ told me what kind of soup it was and I cried. After that, I remember not being able to eat much of anything. I think I had rice or anything I recognized as "safe" for the rest of the trip, or I would ask before eating it. It was sea turtle soup. I am still upset Mom let me order sea turtle soup. I hated DJ for telling me and was mad at everyone for letting me order it and eat it.

JANUARY 24, 1980

Conception Island diving. We are diving "the wall," and I've only gone deeper than thirty feet a few times. Ever since the first time that my regulator broke, I try staying right next to Dad. I've been cautious, to say the least. Diving the Conception Wall was "a dive not to miss," so I've been told. It's hard to say if I am excited or totally freaked out or possibly both. On the west side of the islands, the ocean floor descends gradually but is no deeper than 2,500 feet, but on the east side—there are steep cliffs down into the ocean—and the North Atlantic Ocean is about two and a half miles deep where the white tip shark lives, the true blue deep water shark…and do you know where these sharks come to eat? Yep, the reefs!

Why is it that I find myself praying to God more often when I am fearful, though I should be praying when thankful for the everyday things like food and fresh water? I hear my name…

Goodbye—for now!

ON MY BUNK, RELIVING THE DIVE
JANUARY 25, 1980

We double-checked all the gear, but I continued to feel my heartbeat pounding like a big bass drum. It was beating so hard, I thought if I looked down at my chest, I could see it popping out like a cartoon character's heart when they see someone they love. My heart was a pounding in my ear. Matter of fact, I am sure that every fish around is swimming to my heartbeat. Yep, I could see it. Several of the giant blue parrotfishes' eyes were on me, and their tails and fins were swishing to the beat.

At only seven feet we started seeing the bright-colored coral all around us. All shapes and kinds, in a rainbow of colors. There were orange sea fans, and they look like a handheld fan the ladies used to hold to fan themselves. Yellow brain coral looked just like a picture I once saw of a brain—weird. The organ pip coral was super cool. They are tall skinny tubes that look like organ pipes. I was expecting music to come out of them at any moment. Funny, right?!

The farther down we swam, the farther we sank into "their" world. We were definitely the visitors, or tourists, down there. The coral heads below us were growing in size and practically glowing with brilliant colors. I haven't seen bright colors like those since last summer when I went to visit Granny. She lives in Las Vegas and driving down the Las Vegas strip with all the neon signs flashing, luring visitors and tourists to come into the casinos, was very bright. Even my grandparent's best friends, Howard and Marie, live in a mobile home park with a blue sign with neon tube lights that read, Tropicana Mobile Park. The coral is far from flashing, but it's bright and beautiful. It's funny how their colors seem to flash like the signs in Las Vegas, but the corals and sea anemones are calling critters and once they are inside, the coral swallows them up! I have never seen this happen, but that's what Dad said happens. What happens in Vegas, stays in Vegas. Same goes with the coral reefs, I guess.

As we descended to about thirty feet, I think, Dad signed for me to look up. Three sharks were cruising along the wall's edge. What a sight from below. I was much more comfortable being below the sharks than above them. I followed Dad and DJ through a tunnel where the reef fish seemed to have doubled in size. The triggerfish were almost twenty inches long, and the blue tangs about ten inches long. We explored more and decided to descend farther down. At about fifty feet below the surface, it's a little darker, as it is harder for the sun to reach through fifty feet of water. The coral seemed to be above us more than below us. We made our way through the outside of this coral "fish town." Caves, tunnels, and overhangs were totally radical. Large grouper fish checked us out, not too bothered with what they saw. Larger stingrays made their way, lobsters peered out from rocks, and turtles swam only about twenty to thirty feet away.

The Wall was just that, a wall. The dark blue deepness adjacent to the wall was the area to the open sea. It seemed to be staring at me, or maybe even calling me. When I looked toward the darkness, it appeared to be empty, but I knew there were large fish eyes looking my way. I was merely a small snack they could have grabbed in one swift move. I was hoping I was too dull in color or too scary with these bubbles floating up around me. I now understand the importance of not wearing anything shiny in the water. DJ had his dive watch on and little fish were always trying to jab at the shiny dial on the watch. He thought it was funny. I thought of the larger fish that wanted to do the same thing.

In photographs and paintings, the wall of corals in so many shapes and colors look like interesting rock shapes, but in real life, I saw the living parts. The algae and the coral depend on one another to live, and I saw this living wall, full of color, and their little fingers like ends swaying in the water and opening and closing—eating, I guess. The families of fish were every color, shape, and size that I could ever have imagined. The sponges, sea urchins, sea stars, sea worms, fireworms, shrimp, and snails lived and hunted all over the reef. I didn't even know such bright colors existed under the sea. It was…I have no words…amazing.

I wanted to look for seahorses, but they stay in more sheltered areas. I did find queen angelfish and a pufferfish and followed a squid until Dad told me she would ink me. But I couldn't seem to help myself from looking over my shoulder, out into the open water. I noticed several sharks near and wondered if they were there before or more were coming around. They didn't seem to care that we'd invaded their territory, or at least that's what I was telling myself.

I am trying to remember all the things I saw and what was my favorite, but I liked everything. There was a stingray that made a grand entrance. As swiftly as he glided near us, he was gone just as fast. We had turned back and started ascending, the words we have to use diving so I can get used to them and pass my written test. When we started going back up to the surface at a slow easy pace, the coral seemed to get brighter as the sun's rays made lines through the water. Algae need warm water and sunshine to live, so the shallower we dove, the brighter the coral. A giant blue parrotfish followed us up, probably making sure we were leaving his "coral town." I didn't know there are thirteen different kinds of parrotfish until today. The bluehead wrasse was male and all the little yellow and white fish were the females. He is like ten times the size of the girls. There are more of these fish on the reefs than any other kind, even the parrotfish!

Did you know sea stars (starfish) could be blue? I thought they were all orange. I watched the blue sea star today closer than I have ever watched one. I noticed his beautiful blue color and the way he moved across the coral rock. He was using his suction cup like feet and five legs in flowing dance motions. So totally cool. He seemed to be going someplace, so I watched him longer than Dad and DJ wanted me to. His little feet continued to move in a marching type way, fast but flowing. He inched his way toward a sea snail, hovered over it, and hunched up. I watched as the sea star ate the snail. It was awesome and totally gross. The sea star grabbed hold of the snail with his little suction-cupped feet and pried the little critter's shell open, and his stomach dropped down and swallowed the critter. The snail was gone. I about puked, but I couldn't— I had a mask on! When his dinner was done, the sea star's stomach went back inside and the empty shell dropped. This must be how a sea star can eat big shellfish. They digest it before they retract their stomachs back inside their body. Crazy, totally gross, and totally gnarly!

A gurgling yell had broken through the sound of my regulator. That was how DJ got my attention. He signed, "look up." A sea turtle swam right above me. Her belly was a soft yellow, the color helping disguise her from things looking up at her from below. It was cool, because when I first looked up, I didn't see anything but the ocean's surface. But when found her, she was just gliding along. Her flippers moved easily through the water, sort of like paddles. She had an olive skin color, which now makes me realize she was a green sea turtle. How cool would it be to be able to swim as fast as thirty-five miles per hour, hold your breath for hours, and travel thousands of miles a year? Just swimming around with the sea currents, like the sea turtles do. This turtle had a fan club that followed her around. Several little yellow tang fish were eating the creatures and mossy-like stuff that had planted themselves on her large shell. Maybe she was here for a cleaning.

Dad had to tell me what the sponges were when we got back. They were so colorful. They aren't the type of sponges we use to wash the dishes, but some people "harvest" these sponges to sell. So, people use them, but when the sponges die, they turn an ugly brown color. They don't keep the bright colors I saw on the reef.

The reef had so many colors, like purple, yellows, reds, pinks, blues, oranges, and more. Oh, and there are several things down there you want to touch or feel but can't! Gloves couldn't even protect you from some of the poisons and sharp things on reefs. It's beautiful, but if you touch or move it, some of it will die or kill you. These are some of the first warnings Dad and Mom taught me before snorkeling on reefs in California.

I could hear my dad's words echo in my thoughts when I was diving. "Never beat your bubbles up to the surface." The condensed air in the tanks do something to your body, making it extremely dangerous because something with the oxygen in your body will expand too fast if you go to the surface too fast. I don't understand it all, but I don't want to die! So we swam slowly and stopped several times to watch as the sharks cruised by, or someone would point out another cool fish or a lobster peeking out of his hiding spot in the coral.

When any grouper was spotted below us, DJ pretended to spear him as he did several other fish too. That would have been crazy to spear a fish with so many sharks around. The scent of blood would have sent the sharks to us in a flash, and we would be there for their feeding frenzy. Thankfully, it was pretend.

The coral began to lose its bright colors as the water temperature got warmer, but it was still beautiful. I could watch the little clown fishes all day long. Clown fish swam in and out of the anemone, inviting their prey into their "dens" for dinner—their dinner. When the crabs saw us, they backed quickly into their holes, but left their bugged eyes out to watch us. Schools and schools of small fish swam alongside us, darting away and then sneaking back to our sides for another brave look at us.

When we reached the surface, we switched our regulators out for snorkels, shut off our air tanks, and headed toward the dinghy. No need to waste tank air for a short cruise along the surface to the dinghy. I have a funny habit of gasping for air as if I were holding my breath the entire time scuba diving. I think it's a funny little habit, but I am not sure…could be nerves and my being thankful to be breathing real air again. Even though I was a little cold during the dive, I wouldn't have missed this dive for anything, it was so cool!

I must write Laurie and Amie and tell them what I saw. Oh, I have to tell them that I learned a parrotfish poops sand—yes, sand! They poop up to a ton of sand per year. I will have to thank a parrotfish the next time I make a sandcastle!

CHAPTER 11

SAILING SILENCE

FEBRUARY 4, 1980

My stack of letters to Laurie and Amie are creating a storage issue on my bunk. The longer we are out here in the middle of nowhere, the more I doubt these letters will ever be mailed.

Today, I am missing California, my friends, my animal friends, my house, the trail rides, and the food more than normal. I wish we could drive to Chico's and get some veggies and avocados and pick a pomegranate off the tree near the two-stall barn near the house. I wonder if the plums and apricot trees are full of young sour fruit. By now, they should have hundreds, and I can picture the swallows checking on their fruit daily, thinking we planted the trees for them.

Have all the horses made their way to Kentucky yet? Or are they in their nearly regular routines in Rancho? I wonder if HoneyBear remembers me. Do they think of me like I think of them? BabyBear must sense my emotions because it's not often that she comes into my cabin and curls up with me as she has right now. She is such a sweet kitten, and I love playing with her on deck and watching her run and hide.

FEBRUARY 8, 1980

Dad and DJ went out for a deep dive hoping to find a shipwreck. I have no interest in going more than a hundred feet down. If I have learned anything, it's the simple fact that every twenty feet deeper, it not only gets a little darker, it gets colder, and the fish double or triple in size. Their mouths and teeth get larger, and did I say…the water gets colder. Plus, I am growing out of my wetsuit. The top no longer goes down to my waist, the sleeves seem to be three-quarter sleeves, and the chest squeezes me, making it nearly too uncomfortable to move or breath. Once I was in the water, it was better, but the fight to take it off was the last straw. We practically had to cut it off me. When we get to St. Thomas, US Virgin Islands, we will be able to buy a new one for me, but I don't think we will be there for another few months.

Today I plan to finish my last couple schoolwork books, if I can. I am almost done with my schoolwork for the year, or at least what I could get done. If I have learned anything on this boat, I've learned everyone should thank a teacher. It's been challenging to say the least without their help. I don't miss the four-walled classrooms, but the school I attended down the hill for a couple years was far from the typical classroom. Donna and Mike, our teachers at Diegueno Country School, were so nice. We sang songs, learned to play the guitar and piano, and performed plays about things we were learning about. In the art room, or in this case the outbuilding, there was a kiln where we learned to throw basic pots on potters' wheels. Several times I rode Coconut, my black-and-white Welsh pony, to school and tied her to the huge playground set and at break, she was my show-and-tell. Speaking made my gut wrench, and I broke out in a sweat. But talking about Coconut, well, I wasn't alone…she was with me. Plus, everyone loved her, and Coconut was as sweet as a pony could possibly be. It helped that all fingers would still be attached after feeding her carrots, unlike Vicky, who would have had a few finger snacks. After the show-and-tell, I rode Coconut back home. After I put her back in her corral, I walked down the hill and went back to school. Besides Diegueno Country School, the other schools made me feel uncomfortable. I don't know why. The reason I liked the Rancho school was because I was with Amie and Laurie. La Jolla Country Day was a much larger school, at least the classrooms felt huge. The bus ride home was super long, and I had to wait a long time at the bus stop for Mom or Fran to pick me up. Once I started walking home it got so late, and other times, kids on the bus started teasing me because no one was there to pick me up. Anyway, being on the *Western Star* has been the best field trip ever! But please don't tell Mom and Dad I said that!

When Mom tells DJ to do his schoolwork, he slams the books on the table and turns some pages, making it look like he is reading, and when she leaves the area, he quietly puts his books back on the shelf and hides in our cabin. He takes a book in there, just in case she catches him. Last time she yelled through the door at him, and he yelled back that he was reading. She believed him. I don't!

FEBRUARY 10, 1980
LEAVING CONCEPTION ISLAND, THE BAHAMAS

It seems as if everyone has joined me up on deck this morning.

My hair is extra curly today because the air is thick

with moisture. Everyone is watching the clouds as they build up taller and darker off in the distance. It feels like the calm before the storm; the birds are quieter, the water below our hull is darker, and the morning sun is fading. New clouds appear to be popping up around us casting darker shadows everywhere, while the tall, dark, and not-so-handsome ones are looking scarier by the minute. Thank goodness they are off in the distance…at least a little, but my hair curling up is a sign the clouds are closer than they appear. Dad and Captain John decide on making a run for it. Yep, we are bringing up the anchor and will try and race away from the storm. The storm that could easily push a sailboat up on shore.

DJ is uncovering the mainsail. I'd better dash below deck to put away anything left out and secure all of the doors.

8:05 A.M.

We rushed to secure everything before we had the anchor all the way up. Mom scurried about from one area to the next and then off to the aft cabin to store any supplies left out. We hardly had the anchor up when Dad just put her in gear and is heading us out to sea. Mom took over the job of securing everything in the galley and everywhere else below deck. I don't think I have ever seen her move as fast as she did today, and she didn't even notice I stopped working and sat at the table to write. The footsteps are heavy and quick up on deck, and I can hear the winch followed by the flapping of the halyards and the mainsail as the sails are being raised, along with the growl of the diesel engine. We are hardly out of the bay, and I can feel the swells of the seas already.

I'm needed up on deck to help and well, maybe not get sick here below deck!

10:13 A.M.

The wind was chilly and damp while we raised the sails; it took more strength than usual. Normally I can crank a winch and hold a line, but not today. Today the guys had to do it themselves. The wind filled the sails and swished us away from Conception Island. The swells are choppy and growing larger, rocking the boat more than we have had in a while. Mom headed off to the aft cabin, her favorite place in rough weather, though she pops up on deck for short visits and fresh air, and then goes below again. DJ likes to hang out on the aft deck, and Dad and Captain John are usually in the cockpit or looking at charts or in the engine room working on something. I am typically on the bow, but I expect these swells, the rolling waves, and rain will keep me here in the cockpit today.

We are safe away from the coral. Conception Island is now in our past.

12:23 P.M.

SAILING. CONCEPTION ISLAND TO LONG ISLAND IN THE BAHAMAS

We are sailing around the storm, making our way to Long Island, The Bahamas. It's still rough, but the rain is off in the distance.

With the wind in my face, I closed my eyes and listened to what I call sailing silence—the wind blowing and the slight crinkling, crackling, and popping of the sails. The halyard lines running up the mast make a loud ting or clank sound with every pitch and roll of the hull. The splash of sea water across the deck adds another sound layer, each unique depending on where the water spray lands. As the spray hits fiberglass, the water sounds like a patter. Splashing the teak and the canvas Jet Ski covers adds a putter, and the porthole covers make the sound of a pitter. Sailing silence is music only a sailboat on the open sea can make. It can put you to sleep like a lullaby or awaken you with a sudden jolt, like the end of an orchestra's grand finale.

However, this girl must go get a blanket—it's cold up here on deck!

This reminded me of the orchestra concert we'd attended in Santa Fe. I had curled up in the seat leaning against Mom's arm and fallen asleep to live classical music. Near the end, the music woke me as if each instrument blurted out, "Wake up!" I watched the conductor's arms flapping like a bird's wings in a storm. The higher his arms, the louder the music. The faster he moved his arms, the faster the instruments played. I was shocked how they could follow his crazy arms slower, faster, louder, and softer.

Sitting here on the *Western Star*, we are somewhere in between nowhere and someplace. Today's music is conducted by Mr. Cumulonimbus and sponsored by Mrs. Mother Nature.

Thankfully we missed the storm; now I am enjoying the ride.

7:05 P.M.

During the last tack, a few things jumped over the small railings that are supposed to hold items on the shelves down below. I quickly ran down the steps and tucked them away since I needed my jacket anyway, then made my way back up on deck. Everyone was sitting in the cockpit, watching the storm clouds and trying to read what was coming our way. The thing about tropical storms, or afternoon storm showers, is that they can pop up from no-where, causing danger to anything in their path, and this can happen at any time, within a moment's notice. This can happen on land too, but when at home (on land), we can hide in a basement. On the boat, we have nowhere to hide. A storm can sink a boat, and in a storm, our sixty-three-foot tall mast seems like it's daring lightning to strike it. This storm could have easily pushed the *Western Star* into the coral or up on the beach because Conception Island wasn't large enough to be much of a shelter.

The mainsail gives a sudden humph as the wind shifts directions and then finds the sails again. With only the mainsail and the jib up, the wind is gaining strength. The only sounds are the wind rolling off the sails and the bow dancing and splashing through the waves. Sailing silence has made me very sleepy.

FEBRUARY 11, 1980
LONG ISLAND IN THE BAHAMAS

We must have sailed around the south end of Long Island while I slept. The storm has passed us, but there are still lots of clouds in the early morning sky. We are in shallow water. Even though I fell asleep, this day seems to be getting longer. Eight hours of sailing out at sea can sometimes feel like only an hour on a beautiful day, but an hour can seem like several days in bad weather! This morning has already lasted for more than a day, it seems. Currently, it's peaceful, and we're heading on a northerly course. As we approach Long Island and make our way around the north end, we will follow the leeward side of Long Island to Stella Maris Marina.

Planting myself down in the cockpit after enjoying some time on the pulpit, I could hear Dad on the hand-held ham radio asking for help. He was speaking with a taxicab driver on Long Island whose cousin has a skiff and was apparently heading out to guide us in. We continued this back-and-forth pattern until the Bahamian skiff was spotted, and then were ordered to douse the sails. After the sails dropped, we tightened and secured the boom, rolled the ropes, and started putting the canvas covers on the sails as the skiff pulled up to our hull. The man spoke with a weird accent I couldn't really understand. He had very dark tanned skin and nodded to Dad a lot. His friend or cousin jumped from their skiff up to our deck in one quick move. Dad stood near the pulpit as another stranger boarded the *Western Star* and headed to the pulpit to help. I'm just thankful they aren't pirates!

It seems the nautical charts are all wrong after Hurricane David made a mess of the sand reefs, canals, passageways, and inlets. We inched our way over the coral beds and reefs under motor. I knew we were over coral because everyone could see it from the deck. It was clear, calm water like Cat Island with a hint of Maya blue color mixed in, the color of my room back home. The only movement was our boat's hull through the schools of fish. Captain John followed the directions of the man in the skiff and the strangers on our pulpit. The four of us stared at the astonishing sight below our keel, as they waved arm signals back to Captain John to turn one way and then the other. DJ and I started rolling lines, straightening up, and securing everything on deck as the *Western Star* putted her way to Stella Maris Marina. The depth finder and sonar were not happy! Yelling beeping sounds constantly warned us of the shallow waters below. Then we stopped on top of sand, and Dad turned off the depth finder and sonar warnings. We would have to wait for high tide to move any farther. He pulled and twisted at his beard, and we didn't dare ask a single question. We sat and waited.

Two hours passed and finally the *Western Star* was released from the sandbar. Dad started her engine, and it grumbled as we made our way to the canal entrance of the Stella Maris Marina. Dad gave each one of us an order to grab the oars, paddles, gaff stick, anything with a reach, and we were to push off the sides of the entrance wall as we made our way inside. Once we managed to pull up next to a dock, we tied off and headed for the restaurant. No one spoke the entire time, and we ate dinner in silence.

I'm sleeping in my cabin because of the man-eating mosquitoes on Long Island. Mom said I have more welts on me than ever. Welts on top of welts. More than I ever had even when we lived in Belize when I was two. I am allergic to mosquitoes, so one bite leaves me with a huge welt, itchy and swollen, and I have to take medicine. It's not fun. Plus, I scratch them open in my sleep, leaving me with little bloody wounds that fish like to strike at in the water.

FEBRUARY 12, 1980
SAILING TO THE ISLAND OF HISPANIOLA

At high tide, Dad cranked the motor. He couldn't leave Long Island fast enough. He said he hadn't slept a minute because during low tide, the boat was actually resting on its keel in the harbor. That is incredibly dangerous for a sailboat, so I didn't want to hear more. We didn't head south like we'd planned, but instead made our way north. The way we sailed in was the way we would sail out.

As we made our way to the windward side of Long Island, we set a course heading for the island of Hispaniola. We will sail the Old Bahama Channel for about two days before we see land again. Two days IF the wind stays about the same. It all depends on how much wind will fill our sails. And if I'm setting our course headings or not. It's tempting to give it a try because it's been months and months since I've had any Chinese food!

I'm so funny. I really need to get off this boat.

FEBRUARY 14, 1980
PORT DU CAP-HAITIEN, HAITI, ISLAND OF HISPANIOLA

We are definitely not in The Bahamas anymore! The sandy beaches and flat islands are behind us. Here the coastline seems to go on and on, much like Baja California. More huts than houses can be seen from offshore, and several bright colored skiffs line the beaches with fishing nets laid out, I guessed to dry. Large mango trees and palm trees are all over the place, and the landscape went from cliffs to beaches, then beyond the beach to a rolling hill with thick forests. Plants cover the hills down to white sandy beaches, and as we sailed the cliffs grew, reminding me of the cliffs around California, but not so dark and jagged. The waves crashing onto coral below the cliffs was definitely not an area for surfing or swimming.

I noticed everyone was on deck as we followed the shoreline before arriving in the Cap-Haitien harbor, Haiti.

We have been sailing for two days, land looks really good to all of us.

Scary warnings on the charts for boats entering Cap-

Hatien harbor read something like this: Warning. Harbor entrance dangerous, numerous reefs in area. Cloudy water. Channel lightly marked. Dock tie up to visit Port Captain.

Dad told me to put modest clothes on, that my bathing suit and cover shirt wouldn't do. He added another "order" that I had to wear a hat with a pony tail, plus lock up Baby-Bear in the aft cabin. "Why?" I asked, but he didn't answer. I was down below when we reached the fuel docks, and I heard men speaking in French or something like French. I didn't know. Mom said that Haiti is full of history and the people are of French and African-Caribbean descent. So, that could be the mix of language they were speaking. She told me this country is about the size of Maryland, but I honestly don't remember how big Maryland is. I didn't ask either, or she would make sure we added that to my schoolwork. Mom also said that the people from Haiti started leaving in small skiffs and would load them with twenty or more people and then try to make it to the United States. No one has a job or money, so they have to leave. If they are piling people into small skiffs and heading to the United States, they must be desperate. I couldn't imagine any of it. I have a hard time on a fifty-three-foot boat with five people.

When I went up on deck, there were a couple of young men arguing on who would help Dad and Captain John with the fuel. I couldn't understand a word they were saying, but the arm gestures and their voice levels told the whole story. A moment later, I could feel their eyes watching me. I was hoping I was wrong, but I wasn't. They were staring at me. Uncomfortable! I was not sure what to do. I sat in the cockpit and pretended not to notice. After the customs people wanted to board the boat, Mom came up and the four of us left the docks. We left Captain John in charge of the four customs people.

We walked along the main road to shops where I saw children much younger than I am running around without parents. Most of the little kids were naked. The kids that were about seven had underwear or shorts on, and the nine- and ten-year-old kids had either shorts or the girls had what looked like old and faded, once-colorful pieces of material tied around their bodies like dresses. These cute little kids walked alongside us, holding their hands out toward us, saying something in French-Creole. They were using their hands to gesture; with one hand they pointed at our pockets and then would point to their cupped hand. Over and over again. The cupped hand was reaching out as if we should fill it with something, like money. Eventually they gave up and ran off to play in the streets. There weren't any cars driving around, so they were safe, I guess.

Dad told me if you give them anything, more will come, and they will become angry you gave to one and not everyone. When we would sail down to Cabo San Lucas on the *Sharon Ann*, the people there were trying to sell us items like shells, shell necklaces, bracelets, and cloths they had made with bright flowery prints. In Haiti, they only begged. I now realize why Mom and Dad didn't give me any money. I would have given those little naked, dirty kids every dime I had in my pocket.

As we walked back to the boat, I noticed several older dark-skinned women with dark black hair walk past me, and then they would walk beside me. They kept bumping into me, even though we had the whole sidewalk to ourselves. It was actually freaky. After a while, I figured out why. They were touching my hair. It had fallen down my back, out from under the hat. Dad must have noticed because he stepped back and began to walk closer to me, draping his arm around my neck. It was a hot, muggy day, and I didn't want an arm on me, but it kept them away from me. If I'd only known, I would have made sure my hair was tucked under my hat. It was so strange. Why would people want to touch someone's hair?

That night Dad had invited the four men in uniforms to dinner on our boat. I recognized the port captain and the port authority's chief of police right away, but the other two seemed to be important people because of their official uniforms. They spoke broken English, but for the most part, it was understandable. They asked Dad several questions about our voyages, and he told more stories of our trips down Baja than our current voyage. The port captain told him to not let us leave the docks without someone to watch over us, like a bodyguard, and suggested a one for each of us if we were staying past tonight. After today, with the women wanting my hair and the men staring at me, I was comfortable with finding bodyguards.

The next day, shopping with the bodyguards was much nicer, and they took us to the best places. We visited a marketplace where they sold fresh fruit and handmade items. It was as if we were in a different town from yesterday, but really it was only a few blocks away.

Every day, some nice local fishermen visit the boat after a day of fishing. Dad loves it and has made a couple friends, and the fishermen are making extra money. Dad has been buying lobster and fresh fish every night. The past couple days have been so much better than the first day. Maybe it's the guards. Everyone we have talked with seems very nice.

FEBRUARY 20, 1980

It's been a busy week exploring in Haiti. Well, mainly shopping. It's so hard not to buy everything, even the little stuff Mom calls junk. She let me buy some little sticks you can bang together and make music with, that have Haiti painted on each one. I wish I could have bought a few other things, like the woven hat was cool, but Mom said it would mold on the boat. I want to help these people in Haiti make money so they can support their families, but I don't have any money, and Mom will not buy "junk," as she put it.

Today's treasure was when we found the red avocados. Red-skinned avocadoes! Mom and Dad had never seen them before either. But we love avocadoes, so I can't wait to try them!

Our chores have been cut down to only a few because no one should ever touch this harbor water! We were up on deck doing little jobs when Captain John yelled for us to come up on deck. A sailboat was heading into harbor and had missed the channel completely. We found out the channel is only about twenty feet wide, but they were not even near the cut. The sailboat's keel was exposed, and her sails were fluttering in the wind and slapping the water. It was terrifying! That could have been us! We could see the people moving around, getting into their dinghy, and after a while they left her there. The sailboat sat all alone on the coral beach with the small waves crashing onto her hull, her sails now lying in the water. I worried about the people, but I cried for the sailboat. As much as the *Western Star* has meant to me, I couldn't imagine leaving her on the coral reef like that.

Hours later, we spotted local skiffs around the wrecked

sailboat. Her broken hull is so sad. The locals from the skiffs climbed on board. They made trips or it was a lot of different skiffs, I wasn't sure. We watched them as they took beds, cushions, fishing poles, the wood cabinets, and the stove. Skiffs filled with items continuously scooted away as it became darker and darker. We could see lights, maybe flashlights, throughout the night. Thieves worked like little ants removing lines, cleats, winches…they even took the sails and the railing.

In the morning, the poor boat was bare. Whoever they were, anything and everything was gone. The only thing left was her hull and the mast. I think the mast is still there, but I can only see her keel from here. The local fisherman friend my Dad made told us before he left fishing that the sailboat didn't have one cleat, one bit of hardware left on her, everything was gone. All that was left was her broken hull, the skeleton. Most people don't know this, but a hull looks like a rib cage under her fiberglass skin, so this makes it even more sad. It was strange that we never saw the owners or heard anything about them. I wonder if that's what we would have done, packed a bag like the one we arrived with and grabbed BabyBear and left the *Western Star* up on the coral reef.

FEBRUARY 22, 1980
CITADELLE HENRI CHRISTOPHE

A visit to the fortress; Citadelle LaFerrari (Citadelle Henri Christophe). This was top on Mom's list of things to do in Haiti, so the four of us made a day of going to the Citadelle. Lucky Captain John stayed behind with the boat. The Citadelle was about a twenty-minute car ride outside of town. A guide drove us, and I thought we were going to die because he drove worse than DJ would have! We stopped at a path that went up to where the Citadelle sat on top of the mountain, then walked up the never-ending uphill trail that was four miles but seemed like twenty. It was easily five miles straight up! A long walk, uphill and in the heat; it felt even longer than twenty minutes, and my feet and legs are killing me.

When we reached the top and I first glanced at the citadel, it was totally rad. Fortress- and castle-like, a fairytale could be created within those walls. Huge old stone bricks made the super tall walls that were probably twenty feet high. The steps started about fifty yards from the doors and went up the rest of the pathway to the opening. The doors are missing and the walls are bare, but the grandness of its frame and structure mean it doesn't take much to envision its once greatness. The opening had to be where doors had hung. Huge cannons sat everywhere. I think there were hundreds of cannonballs at each corner and piled near the openings where a cannon belonged. Every wall we followed had cannons, and they were every size imaginable. Some were aimed out the windows, ready for battle. Looking out from what I would call a window in our house, but these didn't have frames or glass, I could see for miles and miles. On the ocean, at sea level, I can only see (or any person can only see) about three miles or less until it looks like the Earth falls off, but up there, I think I could have seen farther than five miles! It reminded me of when I would ride to the top of the hills on my trail rides, but here, I couldn't ride unless I found a path. The only path I saw was the one I walked up, but riding a horse up that hill would have been awesome. The plants and trees were everywhere, and it would take some time to create paths through that thick stuff.

We walked through some of the building and visited the dungeon. I didn't like it at all, and my hairs on my arms stood up. We moved into rooms where they must have stored food and water. I wonder how long they waited for their enemies; enemies that Mom said never arrived. Most of the building didn't have a roof. I am not sure if it fell or if they didn't build one. It was very muggy and hot up there. The mosquitoes wanted to carry me away. Most of them munched on me, so I spent most of my time killing them. When Mom and Dad finally noticed I was covered, they decided we could go. Mom looked upset that she couldn't stay longer. I felt bad, but I couldn't wait to get back on the boat. I'm still in pain! My own curse—allergic to mosquitoes.

FEBRUARY 24, 1980

Dad surprised DJ with his late but promised Christmas gift. I'm a bit jealous. It's a French-made windsurfer, the D4, and I didn't want a windsurfer but I would like to try it out. DJ can't wait to use it, but Dad said it will have to be tied on deck until St. Thomas unless we go someplace like a nice beach to anchor out for a few nights, but our plan is San Juan and then St. Thomas. What a bummer, dude!

FEBRUARY 25, 1980
LEAVING PORT DU CAP-HAITIEN, ISLAND OF HISPANIOLA

As we left Port du Cap-Haitien, there were a couple cargo ships docked, and one had left just before us, making it easier to follow the cut out safely. I don't remember the cargo ship docks coming in, but maybe I was below deck. Mom told me Haiti exports coffee, mangoes, sugar, rice, and other things. I don't remember all of the things, and I am not going to ask because it will turn into another lesson. She also told me that in the 1700s, or the eighteenth century as Mom calls it, Haiti was becoming a rich country. But after they didn't allow slavery in the late 1700s, Haiti didn't do well because they had to pay the people to work. It was a very stinky, dirty harbor and town, besides the 1820 Citadelle built on top of the mountain near the town of Milot. Milot was a tiny town. It had hut-type houses and not very many of them. I saw people outside on the street, going about their day and walking from shack to shack carrying baskets. The small kids were naked, and the older kids had clothes but not like the clothes we wore in the States. It wasn't stinky; much like the harbor, the odor was harsh, beyond dirty water and trash.

Mom told us that Haiti is actually one third of Hispaniola Island, and the other two-thirds are the Dominican Republic. One island, two countries, and it doesn't sound like they like one another at all. I wonder if the other side of the island, the other country, is as poor. I hope their harbor doesn't stink as bad as this one did.

We passed the broken hull of the sailboat that ran aground about a week ago, and all of us stared at her. It was if we observed a moment of silence to honor her, or we were all thanking God that wasn't the *Western Star*. Either way, we passed her watching the small waves crash up against her hull, pounding her into the dark coral.

8:00 A.M.

SAILING. PORT DU CAP-HAITIEN, HAITI TO PUERTO PLATA, THE DOMINICAN REPUBLIC, ISLAND OF HISPANIOLA

Ahhh...the open sea! Being back out on the water was like heaven to my nose. It was a sad feeling being in Port du Cap-Haitien. Not the sad feeling like we had to be there, but a sad feeling for the people living there.

Back on deck and leaving the port, with the fresh

sea breeze flowing over my body, feels so good. It was so hot and stuffy in Cap-Haitien, it's nice to feel the breeze and erase the smell from my nose. I wish we could do something to help this country and its people. I will never forget the looks on the kids' faces and how dirty they were playing in the streets. I probably won't forget the port captain either. At first, the officials from customs scared me to death when he demanded our boat be boarded by the customs agents. I guess when going into another country, they have the right to board your boat for anything. I guess they look for weapons, drugs, and other illegal things being transported into their country. But after he was nice and told Dad how to help us be safe, that was nice.

I forgot, the Citadelle. It was cool and the view from its fortress windows was cool, but the mosquito bites are still with me, and unfortunately the medicine makes me sleep a lot. Maybe one day I will outgrow being allergic to mosquitoes like I outgrew being allergic to milk. I wish we had milk. Not the powdered milk we have to mix with water—it's totally gross.

FEBRUARY 26, 1980

1:18 P.M.

PUERTO PLATA, THE DOMINICAN REPUBLIC, ISLAND OF HISPANIOLA

We followed the channel into Puerto Plata, the Dominican Republic. Off our port side was what looked like a small castle, but as we sailed closer, we saw it was a fortress. DJ and I started betting on who would start telling us about history first when we were nearing land, an island, or a lighthouse. We started this game around mid-Eleuthera Island; I chose Dad on the arrival at Cat Island. I won because I had a hint that there were pirates in the area, and Dad knows his pirates! The game became an official game after that, right before the land sighting of Conception Island. Today, DJ chose Mom, and it was Mom who started, so DJ won.

Mom said it was Fort San Felipe del Marrow, or also called the Fortaleza San Felipe. Why two names, I guess I will never know. Ships had to sail past it to enter the harbor, so the fortress walls might have been intimidating to those who entered. Especially since it had cannons pointed at their ship. If ships tried to avoid the fortress, they would see their last day afloat for sure, but not because of cannons. The waves would crash them onto the coral reefs and splinter their hulls into tiny bits against the coral. If pirates found the channel, or the cut, into Puerto Plata's harbor, the little fortress sits right on the entrance patiently waiting to fire its cannons. On the ocean side, the fortress looked smaller because it was built on the harbor side, and you could only see part of the building. It makes sense to me that pirates would see a little fortress and think if they could get close enough, they could fire their cannons at it and demolish it, but then they wouldn't see the reef. If they followed the cut thinking the fortress was little and couldn't do much damage, they would sail around the corner and see the fortress was much larger, and it would be too late to turn around. I am glad it's 1980 and not the late 1500s!

The fortress seems to grow at least double in size as we make our way around the cape, making my story seem more real than I thought possible. The channel wasn't that wide, maybe seventy feet, and back then it would have been much smaller. Between the coral sides and thin channel, no old sailing ships would be able to turn around.

Either way, the ship would sink. My mind always wonders to the what-ifs… What if we were being shot at? What if we lived back in that time? Crazy, right!

We motored safely past the fortress—no cannons fired—and tied up at the customs dock, where Dad took all of our passports and paperwork to the office and got our passports stamped. After they were done, he was followed by the customs officer back to the *Western Star*, and they spoke with Captain John and Dad on the dock. Again, I couldn't understand a word that was spoken, but the tones and hand gestures were enough for me to know it was official. And no, they didn't appear to be happy. A lot of pointing was happening.

Even though Haiti and Santo Domingo are on the island of Hispaniola, they don't share the same language or anything else, according to Mom. Bartholomew Columbus discovered this island for Spain in 1496. I bet Christopher, his brother, was jealous.

Mom left us and joined in the conversation with Dad and the customs officers because she speaks Spanish better than any one of us. But it didn't look like she was helping much. She had said that the "dialect" is very different than what she speaks or can understood.

A few years ago on the *Sharon Ann*, we were sailing back from Mexico and when we arrived back in San Diego, customs boarded us and ordered everyone off the boat. They didn't just look around our boat in San Diego, they carefully searched our boat! All the mattresses on all the beds and seats and couches were all lifted up and pushed aside. They looked inside every storage bin and closet, and didn't shut or put back any of the hatches or covers. They even took the anchor line out of the anchor locker and left the line everywhere in the V-berth. We had been through customs several times, but these officers thought we were hiding something. The thought of customs has made me nervous every time we've been boarded since then. Dad said since the customs people basically tore our boat up, we needed to clean every compartment before we organized them and put everything away. It took us forever. I had no idea a boat could get dirt in a place that can't see the light of day. And it looked like we'd spilled gallons of salt everywhere. Dried salt was on top of, under, and inside everything. It would have been easier to hose her down inside and out. Thank goodness I was so young and didn't have to do too much, but if they were going to do that here, I was not looking forward to cleaning the entire *Western Star*.

I stood wondering if customs was going to tear up the inside of the *Western Star* like a hurricane. We are in a foreign country; anything could happen. My mind was filled with negative thoughts. What was going to happen here in Haiti? Was BabyBear hiding? Poor girl didn't know what was happening, and actually, I didn't either. But after a quick look around, the customs men popped back on deck, shook Dad's hand, and everything seemed great. Dad even invited them to lunch the next day.

MARCH 6, 1980

We've been stuck in the Puerto Plata harbor for about a week now. The seas are rough, so leaving is out of the question. Ships have been reporting ten- to fifteen-foot swells all the way to San Juan, Puerto Rico, which is our next stop. Mom has been trying to call her cousin who lives in Santo Domingo, which is on the west, or Caribbean Ocean, side of Hispaniola. I know she would love to see her cousin. Plus, getting beaten up by ten- to fifteen-foot swells is not what her doctor ordered.

Mom was able to reach Helen, and she can't wait to see us! It looks as if Mom and I will be on a bus for about four hours. That I didn't know! I would rather stay on the boat. After our day or two visit, we will fly to San Juan from Santo Domingo.

Dad, Captain John, and DJ will take the *Western Star* along the remainder of Hispaniola, then cross the seventy-nautical-mile stretch between islands to cross the Mona Passage. Then they will follow Puerto Rico around to the old San Juan area, where they will be docked near the Coast Guard station. Dad expects us to just find them there. It's a city with a big harbor. What if we can't find them? I want to stay, but I don't want to leave Mom, either.

I have to pack—later!

MARCH 11, 1980
SAN JUAN, PUERTO RICO

How to write in a journal without the journal is more difficult than one would think. Mom made me put my clothes in her bag and then we left quickly to catch the last bus, so I forgot my journal and my letters to mail to Laurie and Amie. This would have been the only place to mail them this whole trip, and I forgot them! Ugh.

It was a horrible trip, and a good trip. I will try and fill in the blanks now that we're back.

It was a long and <u>extremely</u> hot bus ride to Santo Domingo. It was horrid and disgusting! Okay, it was awful! We almost missed our bus, which wouldn't have been a bad thing.

Helen was so excited to see us, and Mom was obviously happy to have someone to talk with besides men and kids. We learned all about Helen's job teaching English in a local school, and she seemed very happy but has plans to move to Miami after the next school year to be closer to her daughter and her family. She cooked us a couple wonderful meals, and sleeping on a couch was even nice! The best part, besides seeing Helen, was taking a shower in a normal shower and letting the water run continually. Not having to wet, wash, and rinse in less than two minutes. Or our normal jump overboard, wash, and go rinse off for less than thirty seconds. I even left the water running while brushing and rinsing my teeth, then I felt bad. Well, maybe not. But it was so awesome not to have to sparingly use a cup of water to wet the toothbrush and rinse my mouth and then have enough water left to rinse my toothbrush. My toothbrush gets all hard and dried up when I don't rinse it out under running water.

I can't seem to stop thinking of the bus ride to Santo Domingo, when I needed to cuddle up next to Mom even as sweat dripped off every inch of our bodies. Every eye on the bus was on us. Every move we made, the locals watched us. Every word we spoke, so we sat in silence the whole way. Was it fear? Was I afraid? What made me feel I had to hide by my mother's side? Or was it because it's so hard for me to talk to anyone—"painfully shy," remember. Was it that? But I wonder if that is how people who are "different" feel in the States? With all the English-speaking or light-skinned people staring curiously at their every move? Staring as if their skin or language being different is scary? Or could they simply be curious? The family on our ranch are from Mexico. I taught the kids English and used to be at their house for dinner more than my own. I loved being with Amelia and Alberto! They left the ranch about a year ago, and that's when Fran and John came. I miss Amelia, Alberto, Victor, and Norma. In so many ways, I felt as if they were family. I remember what Donna and Michael at Diegueno Country Day School would say. It was something like this: "An egg is an egg no matter the color. If you crack it open, the same stuff is inside!" I don't know why I can't get this out of my head, but I hope I can fix myself and not be this shy or scared.

Mom and I took a small plane to San Juan and then a taxi to the harbor. As we neared the harbor, I looked out the window and saw the *Western Star*'s big hull and tall mainmast, followed by the little mizzen mast, sails covered with the blue canvas sail bags, and the Jet Skis on the deck. I wondered where BabyBear was hiding. Seeing the *Western Star* in the harbor was like seeing home after a long weekend trip away. I couldn't wait to be back on board and to see BabyBear. The first thing I did was look for her, and she was happy to see me.

Wait…did I call the boat HOME!?!

MARCH 12, 1980
SAN JUAN HARBOR, PUERTO RICO

Strange what a few days in ten- to fifteen-foot swells will do to a person. DJ seemed happy to see me, in a brotherly way. I wonder how long that will last. He said Dad tied him to the table most of the way to San Juan. I gave him a blank stare to prompt more details. He said the swells were so large and rough that everything was flying around, including DJ. Dad had to tie him down so he wouldn't hit the ceiling or the walls and get hurt or knock himself out. He looked like he might cry, but DJ never cries. He said it was horrible and then walked away.

WOW!

Dad told me he and Captain John kept life vests on and had themselves tied in the cockpit so they wouldn't get tossed overboard. I have never seen Captain John wear a life vest, so it must have been bad. After I asked Dad where BabyBear stayed during the bad seas, I think he lied when he said BabyBear was in her favorite spot—the sink. I only think he lied because she would have been tossed out of the sink. I wonder where she hid when the waves tossed her up. Well, she is fine, doesn't look traumatized from the two days of being thrown around, and looks very happy to see both Mom and me...as she continues to follow my every move. She reminds me of HoneyBear. HoneyBear does—did—the same thing at home, followed me around the house. I wonder if she will ever follow me again.

MARCH 14, 1980

SAN JUAN HARBOR, PUERTO RICO

We are staying docked until Dad and Captain John fix the Onan generators. In the rough water sailing over here, the pounding and shaking of the hull caused a lot of damage. The generator needs continuous water flow to cool itself off. There is an intake hole in the hull and the generator sucks water in, the water passes through or around the generator, cooling it off, and then sends it back out another hole. When I am swimming around the boat, I check out all these holes. Well, after I learned what the two holes on the starboard side were, I didn't inspect those again! Those are the holes from the head. Yep, the poop holes on a boat. The other holes are the intake holes where water is sucked in to cool the engine and one for the water purifier. But Dad had said the intake hole wasn't in the water long enough during the rough seas they had to allow the water to be sucked in, so the engine heat fried both circuit boards to both generators. Without the generators, nothing electronic works on the boat. Like the refrigerator, freezer, air conditioner…

Oh, wait, we don't have one of those air conditioner things. I crack myself up.

SAN JUAN HARBOR, PUERTO RICO

In my bunk—it's as hot as an oven!

Dad and Captain John found replacement parts here in San Juan. I'm not planning on becoming a mechanic or anything like that, but when I was snorkeling, I saw the tiny white holes in the hull and asked Dad what they were. It started the whole explanation of what a generator is and how it works. I might not remember exactly what he said, but if I ask, he will tell me how it works all over again. I appreciate that he knows how to fix things and shares the how-to with me, but after five months of these close quarters I might even be driving myself nuts. So I slide away before Dad can put me to work. DJ is the best at that; I can't figure out how he does it, but he is sneaky!

MARCH 21, 1980
SAN JUAN HARBOR, PUERTO RICO

On deck hiding in the little shade I can find. The sun seems hotter here than anywhere in The Bahamas.

Mom, DJ, and I have been going to the nearby resort while Dad and Captain John fix the boat. DJ and I were lucky enough to use the resort's beach toys. My favorite is a small sailboat called a Sunfish, like the one I sailed at camp last summer. I've been sailing this one around everywhere. It was one thing to follow the herd of Sunfish sailboats at camp, and another to be on the ocean. Currents are a big factor, taking me in unexpected directions, and the wind is much stronger than the breeze we had on the lake where there also were no rolling waves. More to risk out here if I were to capsize. There isn't a camp counselor nearby to make sure I can flip it back over, and the current would probably carry me away much faster with a sail and mast in the water. Sailing all alone, the only sounds are those of the waves slapping against the empty, light hull; the wind swishing in the sail; and the small halyard line slapping against the mast. Freedom. When the skiff passed me with a young man waving his arm, telling me to sail back to the beach, that was the only time I remember feeling connected to the world. They had to track me down to get the Sunfish back! But they did have a business and needed to rent it out to the tourists. I could seriously sail it all the way to St. Thomas if Mom and Dad would let me. Maybe not, but I would sure try.

MARCH 28, 1980
SAN JUAN HARBOR, PUERTO RICO

Dad and Captain John finished fixing the Onan generators. They had decided to bolt the circuit boards to the wall instead of putting them back on the generators, to help the problem of overheating and eliminate the shaking They are hoping this will help prevent the circuit boards from frying out again. You guessed it—I asked Dad how they fixed the overheating problem. Really, now I start talking and asking questions…after Dad and Captain John successfully rewired them, and the circuit boards are ready to go.

And so were we! We ended up staying a few extra days, which became a couple weeks. It was because Dad said he was waiting for supplies. The "supplies," when delivered, was a Sunfish sailboat! Merry belated Christmas and birthday to me! My birthday being near Christmas, gifts were always with a card that read: Merry Christmas and Happy Birthday! But this, this is so awesome, I am so happy! I cried! My Christmas and birthday gift—who cares! It's amazing! It was a huge gift! I hadn't been this happy since before we left California. Maybe now I can sail to St. Thomas in my Sunfish.

Dad and Mom ordered the Sunfish with the rainbow sail, and I couldn't be happier with that choice!

We stored the rudder with its tiller and the daggerboard in the aft cabin on the extra bed. The boom and upper boom we wrapped or rolled the mainsail around with the rigging and secured it on the deck. The *Western Star* is starting to look like a floating water toy box. A tow line was secured from the center cleat hitch to the bow handle and through the bow eye and then connected to a cleat on the stern of the *Western Star*.

SATURDAY, MARCH 29, 1980
SAILING TO ST. THOMAS, UNITED STATES VIRGIN ISLANDS

We readied the *Western Star* for the journey to the United States Virgin Islands (USVI), the island of St. Thomas. Dad double-checked the bowline knots tied to the front of the Sunfish in tow behind the dinghy and then double-checked the knots from the dinghy to the *Western Star*.

The Sunfish and the dinghy were bouncing off one another, so Dad decided to tow the Sunfish behind the dinghy.

What a sight to see as we made our way out of the harbor—a huge motor cruiser sailboat with Jet Skis, a windsurfer, a Sunfish mast, and a cat on deck, being followed by a dinghy, and the dinghy being followed by a Sunfish sailboat. I wish I had a photograph of us to mail to Laurie and Amie.

"Today's weather: partly cloudy, with a slight chance of showers sometime, some wind in areas, and mostly sunny in most areas. Swells should be slight, no more than three feet but most swells will be around one foot or less." We've listened to this same weather report on the ham radio for the last couple of days, basically every time we turned the thing on. I think it's a recorded message and they forgot to make a new one—or is the weather like this in the Virgin Islands all the time?

I checked out the charts and, depending on the wind strength, it shouldn't take us long to get to St. Thomas. Between the weather report and the chart, it should be a beautiful seventy-nautical-mile sail!

9:26 A.M.

SITTING AT THE NAUTICAL STATION, WESTERN STAR, SAILING

I've been sitting in my most favorite place on the *Western Star*, her bowsprit. I was there watching the sun rise off our starboard stern. The sun is rising and is warming fast. Soon we will all want to jump off the boat to cool off. White wisps of cirrus clouds splashed here and there and are dashed across the light blue sky. According to the charts, the distance from San Juan to St. Thomas is seventy nautical miles, and we have been going an average of five knots. Our travel time depends on the wind direction and the distance we had to tack, and I don't see that written down, but we only tacked a few times. I think we should still make it there in a few more hours. We left yesterday around dinner, so we should arrive soon.

10:14 A.M.
ON DECK

Just a few minutes ago in the far distance off our bow, the hilly volcanic island of St. Thomas popped out from the dark blue sea. As we sail, the *Western Star* is cutting through the one- to two-foot seas, just as the weatherman predicted. Every minute or so the *Western Star's* hull finds one of the larger swells and smacks down on it, and water sprays across the deck and splashes me! It's cold enough to make me yelp, but it also helps cool me off for a minute. It's as if the *Western Star* is happy to be heading into St. Thomas and playing with me. Strange sounding, but when you're out on the water for seven months, the boat becomes your friend.

DJ sat here for a little while this morning, and it was nice to just sit with him for a bit. I'd never tell him, but I kind of missed him while Mom and I went to see Helen. We never fight while sitting on the bowsprit. We both agreed when we started this adventure that it was the only place on the boat where we didn't have to hear Mom's favorite song blaring from the speakers in the cockpit and made it a safe zone we could share. Over and over again we hear:

"I feel so bad I've got a worried mind. Save a nickel save a dime, working 'til the sun don't shine." Then the singer belts out the next line, and DJ and I run for the hills—or the bow of the boat!

It's actually a great song, but way overplayed on a sailboat, and it's the kind of song that gets in your head and will not leave.

Today might be one of the most beautiful days I've ever seen while sailing in the Atlantic Ocean...or are we in the Caribbean Sea? I know we are somewhere between the two.

Mom made sandwiches for everyone a little while ago, giving me some time to sneak a peek at the charts belowdecks. St. Thomas basically sits where the Atlantic Ocean is to the north and the Caribbean Sea is to the south. We are only hours away from Charlotte Amalie, where we will be docking at Yacht Haven while we fuel up and buy supplies. I don't know what our plans are after that. After that, I walked to the stern and sat on the deck to watch my new Sunfish sailboat as it follows right behind the dinghy. All is well, and I am excited to hop in and sail it around Charlotte Amalie. Well, I hope I am allowed to sail it there.

Maybe it's because of the lack of privacy for the past seven months or the fact that we are arriving at our "final" destination, but everyone is in a good mood while I feel like yelling. Like a good scream would help me release seven months of being angry, anger that seemed trapped inside me, and I don't think I am alone because when DJ found me on the bow pulpit, we stood and screamed song lyrics. After that, DJ and I cracked up, and for the first time, I think we knew we were actually in the same boat!

Being on the boat has been good, but I never stopped thinking of all my pets in California. It's been so long. What if they don't remember me? Lately, I tear up when

I think about my pets and have to make myself do something to get my mind off them.

When we get to St. Thomas, I will finally be able to mail my letters to Laurie and Amie. But now, I am not sure if I will. They are all thoughts from the past and not relevant to today. How I feel today is so much different than what I felt when I got on the plane in San Diego. It's been seven months, but it feels like several years ago. I want my friends. I miss my animals more, and riding…I can't wait to be back on a horse. My life has changed, I can feel it, but I don't know how or why. It simply has.

12:06 P.M.
ST. THOMAS, UNITED STATES VIRGIN ISLANDS

As we make our way around the hilly and very green island of St. Thomas, we see empty beaches and some houses up on the hills. We are entering Charlette Amalie harbor. There is a large hotel up on the cliff overlooking a beautiful white sandy beach. In the harbor on our port side, there are boats tied to moorings, not anchored. I guess this secures a place for each boat, or it could help prevent boats swinging into one another. We are motoring alongside a long dock where a Princess cruise ship is tied. Do cruise ships say, "tied"? We are approaching the docks of Yacht Haven, closing in on the larger boats in the outside slips, and Dad is on the radio now waiting for permission to dock. The dock master speaks English, but his accent is heavy Carib. A few minutes ago, Dad asked DJ to jump in the dinghy and take it and my Sunfish out in the bay. I begged to take my Sunfish out myself, but he refused, so here I am. I just heard them give Dad a slip number, so we are heading toward it now. I have to go grab a line to toss to the people on the dock. Later!

8:39 P.M.
MY BUNK
YACHT HAVEN, CHARLETTE AMALIE, ST. THOMAS, USVI

We were allowed to get off the boat and explore once it was washed and rinsed off and everything was secured, including the dinghy and my Sunfish. But getting off the boat came with an order—DJ and I must stay together at all times. Not the freedom we had hoped for, but we walked down the docks, checked out the marina shops, and hung out for a while. It wasn't long before we noticed several kids around our ages heading toward the docks from the parking lot. School must have let out for the day, because they had their backpacks with them. They walked past us, jumped in a dinghy, and disappeared into the harbor. A few hours later, some of the same kids were back ashore roller-skating around the circle where the car had let them out after school. I watched them from a distance and realized how painfully shy I am. Seriously, it was painful! Desperately I wanted to speak, make friends, but my feet felt as if they were somehow fixed to the ground, my face felt flushed like I had a fever, and my mouth didn't seem to work at all. What has happened to me?

APRIL 1, 1980

Today I made a point of sailing the Sunfish around the harbor about the time the boat kids got out of school. I felt free when I sailed. I went through the moored boats, wondering what boat or boats the kids lived on. The boats were empty and quiet, like everyone was off at work or school. I must have lost track of time because right in front of me was a dinghy with the three high schoolers. Two brothers and a sister…the guys I'd watched skating. In a panic, I lost the wind in my sail and then turned into the wind and became disoriented, tacking several times. Zigzagging and off-balance, I hit a buoy and then skimmed by a boat. I could feel eyes watching me. Heat felt as if it rose from my toes and into my cheeks. All I wanted to do was get back to the *Western Star* and hide in my bunk with BabyBear! I am safe, I didn't crash or sink, but such a coward and a bigger fool. I am so embarrassed. Maybe I will stay here on my bunk forever.

APRIL 2, 1980
YACHT HAVEN, CHARLETTE AMALIE, ST. THOMAS, USVI

I don't want to think about my sailing experience yesterday, but it seems to be swimming in my head. This is the only time I've ever wanted to stay on the boat and do schoolwork since September!

DJ just came into the cabin and told me I had to go with him to the yacht club so he can hang out with his new friends. DJ can't get off the boat without me, so I was forced to go with him. My plan was to stay in the little convenience store near the circle where everyone hangs out and sometimes skates. I plan on pretending to shop or wander around the shopping area. So I went directly to the convenience store and wandered around.

As I stared at the ice cream in the freezer, a voice from behind me softly said, "My favorite is the ice cream sandwich. What about you?" His long tan arm slid over my shoulder as he reached into the ice cream freezer to take one of the bars. I noticed his scent was different, like nothing I've smelled before, and his touch was gentle. DJ would have knocked me to the ground if I were in his way. I looked up at the tall boy standing just behind me; his eyes were as blue as the sky. His blond hair was messy and definitely bleached lighter from the sun. His smile... friendly, which made his eyes squinty. He smiled and said, "Come out and hang with us." He smiled and walked over to the counter to purchase the ice cream bar and walked out the door.

You guessed it...I said nothing! Not one word formed. Not one word could I utter or even mumble. What is wrong with me?

APRIL 3, 1980

YACHT HAVEN, CHARLETTE AMALIE, ST. THOMAS, USVI

Captain John found a boat to sail back to the United States. I guess his job is done here—we made it. I didn't think about what would happen when we got here. It was like he became part of the boat and part of the family. He said he wasn't going to say goodbye, he would say, "Fair winds and following seas," the nautical blessing for good luck and farewell.

I wonder if I will ever see him again.

APRIL 4, 1980

We left the docks and rented one of the moorings out in Charlette Amalie, which made cruising around the docks almost impossible. But every day around the same time, somehow DJ and I made our way to the docks. DJ and I had an understanding of sorts; he wanted to see his new friends, and I want to work up the courage to go with him. I am getting tired of wondering around the stores and watching the divers at the dive shop. I wish I could talk to a human as easily as I can an animal. The kids are like creatures from another world, but maybe I am the one from another planet!

2:50 P.M.

Today I scrounged around to find enough change to purchase an ice cream sandwich, which I didn't really like. I had tried one the other day, and it's not really that good. This time I'm going to face DJ's new friends and not hide.

5:18 P.M.

Do you want to know how it went? Well, I walked up to the group and without thinking just offered the boy with blue eyes my unopened ice cream sandwich. He looked into my eyes, and it was as if the world stopped for a moment. I hadn't even noticed that he reached out to take the ice cream sandwich until his hand touched mine. The ice cream sandwich dropped from my hand, landing in his. When I looked away, I noticed everyone's eyes were on me as I stepped back behind my brother just a bit. Then, to embarrass me a little more, DJ introduced me to everyone as his "little kid sister." I wanted to crawl under a table or hit him, I wasn't sure which one. But I slid backward like a lobster retreating into its dark hole. Nothing I do helps get my mind off it, it's as if it's a bad movie being played over and over in my head. I'm going to go do some schoolwork. Maybe staring at math problems that I can't figure out will help.

6:14 P.M.

I can't get the boy out of my head. It's as if I memorized his face, eyes, hair, and even his hand touching mine reaching for the ice cream sandwich—oh, ya, and his scent. In school I had several boys that were my friends, even some that would come over to the house, and it was more like a brother coming over to visit—well, a brother I didn't fight with, at least. I even danced with some boys at the school dance, but nothing could compare with the feeling I get with this guy.

I don't think it's safe to write this down. I think I have to keep this to myself. I would die if DJ read this or worse—showed it to him!

APRIL 10, 1980

We have been here for a couple weeks, and it has been horrible not to write. I will have to chance it and make sure DJ—or anyone else for that matter—is not be able to find this journal.

It's becoming easier to hang with the "dock-rats"—that's what the kids living on boats in Charlotte Amalie call themselves. They also call Charlotte Amalie "the pit" for several reasons. It stinks, for one thing, but not nearly as bad as Haiti did! The two boys around DJ's age and their sister live on the dark-hulled boat named the DSP. The youngest is who I called blue eyes. He talks to me and makes me laugh, and I have actually been able to speak, although I feel my face warm every time he is near me. I can't seem to control the warming of my face or as they called it, blushing!

Today they talked about the *Sun Princess* cruise ship

coming in on Saturday, as she come's every week or so, and this weekend the "dock-rats" wanted to go aboard the ship and watch a movie or eat from the free buffet. They asked DJ and me to join them. No way! I'm curious but not that brave. I want to go, but I don't want to get caught, nor do I want to figure out how to get back to St. Thomas if the ship leaves port with me. They'd said that once or twice they had to jump off the ship because the gangplank was closed. Diving into the pit's dirty water didn't sound good either, plus the jump would be from a deck that is a few stories high—oh, my! What should I do?

APRIL 12, 1980

It's Saturday! I've been watching the 2,000-passenger cruise ship from up on the *Western Star's* deck all day. The *Sun Princess* looks a lot like the *Pacific Princess*, the cruise ship in California that cruises down from LA to Baja California. It looks like a huge floating hotel, and I almost forgot, *The Love Boat* TV show is filmed on the *Pacific Princess*. I don't know what I expect to see from here, but I will keep an eye on the ship all day if I have to. DJ is with them. He is with the dock-rats—kids we hardly know, doing a crazy thing like boarding a cruise ship.

What if the ship leaves? What if they are caught? How did they got on board? What movie are they watching?

I haven't gone to a movie in almost a year. I wish I were with them!

5:23 P.M.

DJ made it back safe. No one got caught, and I am jealous, and sunburned from watching out for them all day. I read the first three chapters of *Watership Down* a few times and still have no idea what it's about or what I read. My mind was on something else! I wonder if they think I am a chicken for not going. I wonder what they did while they were on the ship. I will have to ask DJ. That's probably a bad idea, but it's killing me not to know.

APRIL 14, 1980
SHOPPING AREA, CHARLETTE AMALIE, ST. THOMAS

Dad is heading to the post office. I am hoping for something from Laurie or Amie. Dad drops us off from the dinghy at the end of the long sea wall that reaches from the Coast Guard station to the seaplane base. Since Mom loves to walk around the shopping areas in Charlette Amalie, where the tourists from the cruise ships go shopping, we are heading there while Dad picks up the mail. Mom and I learned our lesson to not go into town when the cruise ships are in because the shops are crazy, filled with tourists. People everywhere and it's hard to walk down the sidewalks and get into the shops or little restaurants.

It's Carnival week, and Mom said we could come in for the parade! The dock-rats said Carnival week is a blast, but there were no plans on going together to any of the festivities. Or maybe DJ didn't include me in the plans, I don't know. I don't think I want to know. As time passes, the more Dad and Mom let him go with his new friends without me, and I am left to shop with Mom and Dad.

Dad found us after taking his short trip to the post office and handed me one of the larger boxes he was holding. It was heavy, and I couldn't imagine what it could be, but I thrashed it open like a gift on Christmas morning back home in California. Skates! Beautiful new roller skates! The dock-rats roller-skate around the circle and DJ borrows someone's so he can skate. But everyone's feet are much larger than mine. I tried Donna's skates on, but my feet swam inside her boots. I now have my own skates! I didn't have socks with me, but I put them on anyway and skated up and down the road while Mom was inside the shops.

Oh, I was born to skate. Not! I was a complete GOO-BER. Running into the locals—not a great thing to do! I can now understand what they are saying, accent and all! "Get your little white butt off the street with those things," followed by several other comments I won't repeat. A few bruises were made. A little blood was shed. But I have skates! I can't wait to skate "the circle" like everyone else! DJ will not be able to exclude me now!

9:18 P.M.

THE WESTERN STAR, MY BUNK

I completely embarrassed myself today. I can ride a 1,200-pound horse but can't control myself on eight little wheels. I have scrapes and bruises all over and was laughed at more times than I can count. DJ took to it like he's skated his whole life, but I guess that's because he skateboarded or maybe because he is the athlete, I am not! No one wanted to help me because I kept taking everyone out. It was horrible! Dale tried, but he was having fun with his friends and what looked like maybe his girlfriend. And I am sure he didn't want to spend any more time with a dork on skates. Glad it's over for today, and I am looking forward to Carnival…if I can walk after skating.

THE WESTERN STAR, AFTER CARNIVAL
VETERAN'S DRIVE, CHARLETTE AMALIE, ST. THOMAS

Carnival! WOW! There are no words to describe it! Okay, I will try.

Tons of people lined the main street partying, laughing, drinking, and smoking sweet, funny-smelling cigarettes they call ganja or something like that. Calypso bands were playing and by the way, it's my new favorite sound. The parade had music, colorful costumes, and people on stilts walking around, hovering over the people in the crowd. Steel drums "laid out the beat," as DJ put it. There were many instruments I have never seen or heard before. Everyone was dancing and singing, people with dreadlocks, dark people, white people, even white people with dreds— everyone joined in on the fun. It was a massive huge party in the street. After the parade passed, the party kept going, but Mom and Dad made us go back to the dinghy and back to the boat. I can still hear the party from here on the deck of the *Western Star*, but it's too far to watch or see anything. I'm going to bed.

APRIL 19, 1980

It's morning, and I can still hear music and people in the streets from Carnival. Crazy, right but it continues for days. Today I followed DJ and our friends onto the cruise ship. He didn't like having me along, but that didn't matter because I got freaked out, and we ran off together. It was a good thing because a few hours later, we saw four kids jump from the lower outside deck into the yucky water of the pit and swim to their boats. Bad, right?! Totally!

APRIL 24, 1980

DJ and I were able to tell our new friends where we were moving to, and they seemed to know the area. They sail past when sailing to St. John when their parents want to get away on holiday. Holiday, I slowly figured out, meant for the weekend or a vacation, not a holiday like Christmas. I am thankful I didn't ask!

Anyway, they said there is a little island with a beach across the channel from our new place called Christmas Cove, and we should check it out. What a bummer leaving friends—again. I am glad DJ did most of the talking because I was on the verge of crying. It was hard to look Dale in the eyes and not burst out in tears. I don't know if he even likes me—likes me.

5:00 P.M.

This weekend is the last chance I have to go with them to see a movie. DJ talked me into it even though I felt my head was going to explode. The draw was that all the dock-rats were going, including Dale, so we would need to board at different times.

SATURDAY, APRIL 26, 1980, 11:00 A.M.

All aboard!

We picked our fake parents and then followed behind them, lagging enough to let them get on the boat, and then we would tell the people working that our parents had just come on board if we were asked. DJ and I looked more like tourists than the dock-rats, so this was no problem for us. Besides the fact that I must have been green since I felt like I wanted to throw up. Onboard, everyone seemed relaxed, ate, and watched the movie, but I was terrified, couldn't eat, and don't remember one minute of the movie. We made it off the ship before it left for its next port. I was never so nervous in my life.

I guess this was our goodbye adventure—here we come, Cowpet Bay.

APRIL 28, 1980
SAILING TO COWPET BAY, ST. THOMAS YACHT CLUB

We are leaving the pit and heading to St. Thomas Yacht Club on the east side of St. Thomas. Let me repeat—we are leaving! It's as if Mom and Dad don't want DJ and me to have any friends! They picked the farthest place from here to buy a condominium and anchor the boat out in a yacht club. Seven miles away is more than a two- or three-hour walk over steep mountains. I was getting better at skating around the circle with the dock-rats, and DJ and I were invited to a social dance. Sailing my Sunfish has been getting easier, and I haven't run into anything or any sailboat for weeks. I sail past the DSP once in a while to see what is up, and they invited me aboard once. It was nice to meet the whole family. Their parents were so nice and even invited me back for dinner. They didn't seem to mind that I had a huge crush on their youngest son, while my parents… Let's just say this isn't water we have been in before.

7:00 P.M.

At dinner, Mom said she was thinking of taking us to visit the private school on the island and see if we can't finish the school year there. DJ and I looked at each other and at the same time said, "Antilles School?"

This is horrible, even terrifying. I am in middle school, and all my new friends are in high school. They will never stay friends with me. I just want to go back to the States. We would only go kicking and screaming! No way! We both rambled on and on about needing to get back to Kentucky to start riding and practicing for the shows. It seemed like she agreed, but I don't know!

APRIL 29, 1980
ANCHORAGE CONDOMINIUMS, ST. THOMAS YACHT CLUB

The Anchorage condominiums are brand new. We have two condos! One condo to "live" in and one is to rent out to tourists. Dad has decided to charter the *Western Star* so all of our supplies and things must be moved into the condo. Storage on a boat is a whole lot different than a home or a condo, and Mom is having a hard time finding places to put all of the boat supplies. We can hardly walk around in the condo, and she is stressed! DJ and I have been spending time exploring and roaming around the area, but not too far because apparently Mom and Dad think that there are boogie men lurking at every corner. DJ and I are trapped yet again, but this time we can't even jump off the side of the boat and go swimming or take off on the Jet Skis. DJ and I have found some spots we can go without Mom and Dad and the Anchorage beach, where the yacht club dinghies are brought on shore, is my getaway writing place. Mom and Dad can see me from the condo. DJ has been hitting tennis balls and found some people who want to play tennis with him. I sit here—with my butt on the sand near my Sunfish, looking out toward

Christmas Cove, and think about sailing it to Charlotte Amalie.

MAY 2, 1980

I can't believe I am saying this, but it was great while we were on the boat, but now it seems like we are stuck on a weird vacation some place between home and not. I tossed all of Laurie's and Amie's letters and wrote them a couple new letters, but I haven't heard back. It's been months since I have seen them, and I wish I could be with them now. I could use a couple of girlfriends right now, to talk with and share feelings. I wonder if they have boyfriends, I wonder if they are playing sports. I wonder if they are still showing horses. But the thing I wonder about the most is if I will ever see them again.

MAY 5, 1980

ANCHORAGE CONDOMINIUMS, ST. THOMAS YACHT CLUB

Today I got my PADI Open Diver Certification! It didn't take too long and after we dove around Turquoise Bay, we dove a wreck. It was awesome! The instructor was cute but old. He was probably twenty or twenty-three-ish. We had already met at Yacht Haven, but I didn't pay attention to him then. Today we were face-to-face, so it was hard not to notice him, but he wasn't as cute as you-know-who!

I am going to write Granny and tell her what we did today!

MAY 7, 1980

My Sunfish is my only escape, and I have sailed to Christmas Cove every day in hopes that just maybe I will run into a familiar boat from the pit. Somedays I try to see how fast I can get there and back, and on other days, I sail over and swim for a few minutes and then sail back. DJ sometimes windsurfs over, and we swim for a while, but the windsurfer takes a lot of strength and he was always grumpy.

MAY 9, 1980
SAILING TO ST. JOHN'S US VIRGIN ISLAND

We sailed the *Western Star* to St. John's to check that island out. It's a stone's throw away from Cowpet Bay. Okay, not that close, but we hardly had to sail over there. The VHF hand radio was on when I heard, "*Western Star*, *Western Star*, this is the DSP. Do you copy?"

No way! Our friends! My friend!

"Just seeing if you were going to be around Cowpet tomorrow? Over."

"Affirmative, DSP. Over," Dad said as looked over his shoulder at me, giving me a look that I have never received from him before.

I can have friends! I am almost thirteen and a half!

MAY 10, 1980
ST. THOMAS YACHT CLUB BEACH

Today I was hanging out on the beach with Mom, looking out for a familiar boat to sail into the harbor or at least pass by. Hours passed, and there was no dark-hulled boat sailing past with DSP painted in white. By late morning, I kept thinking maybe they'd gotten a late start, or something had come up. I didn't want to leave the beach for fear I would miss the boat. With no phone, it was simply a waiting game. I was starting to feel totally bummed out! Maybe it was time I gave up. So I lay back on the lounge chair, choked back my tears, and closed my eyes.

I felt the sun disappear behind a cloud after a bit, and then realized there wasn't a cloud in the sky today, so assumed it was DJ messing with me, but he and Dad were playing tennis last I looked. I opened my eyes and found a very tall figure standing over me with the sun beaming through his blond hair. A smile from ear to ear squinted his sky-blue eyes. I stayed in his shadow, so I could look up at his face and not be blinded by the sun as I sat up. He asked if I wanted to take the Sunfish to Christmas Cove. I looked around for DJ and thought he would be joining us, but Dale said, "Don't you want to go with me?" I looked at Mom without saying a word, and she actually said, "Sure. Go ahead, you two."

The two of us walked down the beach toward the Sunfish, and he dragged it into the water with such ease. I thought about how hard that small task was for me to do by myself while watching him set the mast into place, and then the sail. He pushed the Sunfish out into the water about two feet and held it while I sat on the edge of the hull and spun myself around, placing my feet inside the cockpit. I thought, *This boy came all the way across the island to be with me.*

He pushed the boat away from the shore, jumped in, grabbed the rudder and the sail line, and when the wind filled the sail, he slid next to me to balance the hull. We sat side by side as he captained the Sunfish toward Christmas Cove.

***

Dear Reader,

I hope you enjoyed reading *Girl Sailing Aboard the Western Star.*

At twelve and thirteen, this was a crazy time to be taken away from life as you know it. What if this happened to you? Oh my!

I would love to hear your story and your thoughts. Would you be so kind as to share with me what you thought about Girl Sailing?

LEFT FOR KENTUCKY IN MAY 1980

The hardest part of living on the boat was being away from the animals. HoneyBear ended up living for 29 years. Vicky died only a few months after arriving to Kentucky because of an accident on the farm. I miss her to this day. Coconut was sold and never made it to Kentucky, and that broke my heart. Not being sure which horses would be sold while we were out at sea, I truly didn't think she would be one of the ones sold. I tear up at that thought, even to this day. Mom had hard decisions to make at the time, I couldn't have made any of them.

While writing this book (editing my journal), I spoke with both of my parents. They had no idea how much I had written, nor did they realize how much living on the *Western Star* had meant to me. At the time, I was full of emotions, including being angry and sad about being ripped away from the things I loved, but as I read my journals all these years later, it all seemed bigger than life. That is when I decided to share it with the world, if the world wanted to read it.

Curiosity got the best of me, and I found the *Western Star* online. She's in good shape! She was recently (2019) purchased and is off to the Caribbean from Florida. I noticed that she still has the teak rails where the Jet Skis sat. The biggest change is the huge canvas canopy covering her cockpit, not the little one we had.

Owing to the unavoidable sun back when we were living on her, I have had over thirty-five skin cancers removed. I didn't baby-oil for fear of sliding off the boat, nor did I care about tanning, but there wasn't sunscreen at that time. Nor did my parents know that at my age, twelve to thirteen, is the highest risk of skin cancer from exposure to the sun. I am fine, lots of checkups and cutting the darn things off of me. But if I can give any advice to you, please use sunscreen!

In 1978 I spent the summer with my new horse trainer, Mrs. Helen K. Crabtree, with her and her talented horse trainer husband, Charles Crabtree, at Crabtree Farm, Inc., in Simpsonville, Kentucky. When I returned to California for the 1978-1979 school year, I had no idea this would be the last time spent in California. After nine months on the *Western Star,* we moved to Kentucky as planned, and I never saw or heard from Amie and Laurie again. I lived in Kentucky for the next five school years and continued to show American Saddlebred horses with the Crabtrees at Crabtree Farms. My horse show life—is altogether another story, along with the answers to the question you might have about blue eyes and what our future had in store for us.

NOTE FROM THE AUTHOR

One thing I couldn't recall or confirm was the yacht's full name or what city the yacht was registered in from the journal entry about Eleuthera's Yacht Club. However, it was from Florida, and there was a side note in my journal that said, MB—Jackie. After some research, I found a yacht built around the year of our trip that somewhat matches the description written in my journal. The yacht *Monkey Business* ended up being a famous yacht because of the presidential candidate Gary Hart and Donna Rice scandal in 1988, but that's not why I used the name. I used it because it was the closest match from my journal. The owner of the yacht at the time had a daughter (I think around my age) named Jackie. This too could be wrong, because there is a possibility that the people I went on the boat with might not have been the owners. Recently I reached out to Jackie on social media but never heard back. She probably thought I was crazy for asking her if she recalled that brief meeting from way, way back when, or maybe it simply wasn't her.

ABOUT THE AUTHOR

RA Anderson is a wanderer who has lived all over, from California to Belize, and currently, home is a town called Rome, in Georgia that is! She grew up on horseback and sailboats—"the most amazing way to grow up!"

A lifelong passion for creative writing and photography became her life. Her award-winning photographs have been featured in table books, magazines, and front-page news, and her writing has been published in magazines, poetry books, and children's books. Her If Pets Could Talk series include: *Cats, Dogs, Farm Animals, and A Service Dog.* Her newest children's series: Iceland, The Puffin Explorers Series includes three books: *Puffins Take Flight, Puffins Off The Beaten Path, and Puffins Encounter Fire and Ice.*

Three boys—her heart and soul—call her Mom. She and her husband—"my strength and passion"—are recent empty-nesters, leaving them more time to travel.

"My life is full, colorful, and exhausting, and I wouldn't trade it for anything. However, people seem to think my most impressive accomplishment is that I know how to work the manual settings on a DSLR camera!"

OTHER BOOKS BY RA ANDERSON

CPSIA information can be obtained
at www.ICGtesting.com
Printed in the USA
BVHW081636130320
574905BV00001B/4